I0610114

Karl Warnke, Ludwig Proescholdt, Thomas Dekker

The Shoemakers Holiday

Karl Warnke, Ludwig Proescholdt, Thomas Dekker

The Shoemakers Holiday

ISBN/EAN: 9783337299606

Printed in Europe, USA, Canada, Australia, Japan

Cover: Foto ©Andreas Hilbeck / pixelio.de

More available books at **www.hansebooks.com**

THE SHOEMAKERS HOLIDAY.

A COMEDY

BY

THOMAS DEKKER.

REVISED AND EDITED

WITH INTRODUCTION AND NOTES

BY

KARL WARNKE, PH. D.

AND

LUDWIG PROESCHOLDT, PH. D.

HALLE:

MAX NIEMEYER.

1886.

INTRODUCTION.

THE earliest known edition of the Comedy of 'The Shoemakers' Holiday' was published in 4⁰ with the title: 'The Shoemakers Holiday. Or the Gentle Craft. With the humorous life of Simon Eyre, shoomaker, and Lord Maior of London. As it was acted before the Queenes most excellent Maiestic on New-yeares day at night last, by the right honourable the Earle of Notingham, Lord high Admirall of England, his seruants. Printed by Valentine Sims, dwelling at the foote of Adling hill, neere Bainards Castle, at the signe of the White Swanne, and are there to be sold. 1600.' Two copies of this edition (A) are preserved in the British Museum, but only one of them is complete (161. b. 1), some leaves of the other being torn away (C. 34. c. 28). "Compared with other plays of the time, the *Editio princeps* of the Shoemakers' Holiday may be considered as rather a careful print." Few passages only offer a faulty construction or an expression, the meaning of which is deficient; throughout the play the versification is smooth and correct; prose may easily be distinguished from verse. ' To all appearance the compositor worked after a good copy of the author's manuscript, and a careful corrector revised the proofs. It is, however, not probable that the author himself passed the play through the press; he would certainly not have failed to put his name, at least in initials, on the title-page, and to correct some of the graver mistakes which occur. "

The second edition of the play (B) was published in 1610. It bears the same title with the *Editio princeps*, only the imprint is different (At London. Printed by G. Eld for J. Wright, and are to be sold at his shop in New-gate-market, neere Christ-Church-gate. 1610). The copy collated by us is preserved in the British Museum, press-mark 643. c. 47. "A number of mistakes being common to A and B, there can be no doubt that B was directly derived from A; cp. II. 1. 26 *a* om., III. 1. 140 *abroade* for *aboarde*, III. 2. 2

eighteene f. *eighteenth*, ib. 4. 1 *O Firke* om., ib. 113 *trust* om., ib. 159 *gentle* f. *gentlemen*, ib. 5. Stage-dir. *his Wife, Sibill in a French hood* f. *his Wife in a French hood*, *Sibill*, IV. 3. 67 *am I* f. *I am*, ib. 4. 19 *me* f. *we*, ib. 5. 28. *mr* f. *your*, and *your* f. *my*, V. 4. 54 *leaue* f. *learne* etc. ' B is, however, not a mere reprint of A, but a revised edition of the play. ⁋ Many misprints and wrong spellings in A are corrected in B; e. g. II. 3. 93 *verstaw* f. *vestaw*, III. 1. 136 *ye* f. *yo*, IV. 1. 101 *dead* f. *deede*, ib. 5. 29 *lies* f. *dies*, ib. 71 *them* f. *then*, V. 2. 45 *you* f. *yon*, ib. 202 *pastimes* f. *pasties*, ib. 5. 23 *Tamar* f. *Tama*. Also the metre has sometimes been smoothed by the addition of some monosyllabic word, I. 1. 41 (*sent*, required by metre and sense), II. 5. 24 (*that*) III. 4. 60 (*now*). Corrections like these have been introduced into our critical text of the play; all other alterations, however, are of a more arbitrary character and must be rejected by us. Cp. I. 1. 193 *come* add. (*lets* disyllable), III. 1. 3 *almond* f. *almonds*, V. 2. 204, 207 *in* om. etc. Neither have we thought fit to adopt spellings like I. 1. 204 *there is* f. *theres*, ib. 207 *my* f. *mine*, II. 3. 18 *you will* f. *youle*, V. 2. 204 *come* f. *comes* (after a plural) etc.

In 1618 a third edition of the Shoemakers' Holiday was published (At London, Printed for John Wright, and are to be sold at his shop at the Signe of the Bible, without New-gate. 1618). Two copies of this edition (C) have been accessible to us, the one preserved in the Bodleian Library (Malone, 226), the other contained in a miscellaneous volume, belonging to the Municipal Library of Dantzic (Comœdiæ Anglicanæ XVII. F. 5. 9). Of the latter Professor Elze, Halle, had a careful transcript made, which he with his wonted liberality put at our disposal. [A glance at the readings of C shows that B was the basis of it.] Common mistakes occur I. 1. 197, 198 *of* f. *in*, and *in* f. *of*, II. 5. 10 (Stage-dir.) *Horner* f. *Horns*, IV. 2. 1 *downe* om. Cp., besides, IV. 5. 137 *pasta* f. *passe*, ib. *pindy-pany* f. *pindy-pandy*, V. 2. 190 *door* f. *doores*, V. 5. 73 *then* f. *them*, ib. 5. 174 *this* f. *feasts*, ib. 197 *words* f. *sportes*, ib. 198 *we* f. *warres*. On the other hand, C offers a number of readings differing from AB. But as most of them are either arbitrary or insignificant, we have fixed upon the reading of C only in those cases in which both A and B are in the wrong.

The alterations and mistakes of C passed directly into the fourth edition of the comedy (D), printed for the same publisher (J on-

don, 1631; preserved in the British Museum, press-mark 643. c. 48).
Cp. I. 1. 33 *me* om., ib. 116 om., ib. 130 some words om., ib. 162
Midasse f. *Midaffe*, ib. 226 *two twopences, to carry into France* f. *three
twopences: two carry into France*, II. 1. 31 *not* om., III. 1. 64 *word* f.
words, III. 4. 125 *goot* f. *groot*, III. 5. 2 *I* om., IV. 1. 88 *not* om.
ib. 2. 12 *Effres* f. *Jeffres*, ib. 4. 45 *father* f. *uncle* etc. In two passages only D has corrected a mistake, overlooked in ABC, viz.
II. 2. 11 *baseness* f. *bareness* and III. 1. 25 *Overies* f. *Queries*.

The last of the old quarto-editions was published in 1657 $\times$ $\times$
(London. Printed for W. Gilbertson at the sign of the Bible in
Giltspurstreet without Newgate). This edition (E) is a bad reprint
of D; even the most glaring blunders have not been corrected; //
cp. I. 1. 145 *a* f. *at*, II. 3. 115 C *eens*, D *oens*, E *ones*, III. 1. 10 *swannekin*, III. 4. 21 *my* f. *any*, ib. 29 *il* f. *ic*, IV. 5. 94 *if* f. *it*, ib. 148
Yet f. *Yes*; besides I. 1. 24 *to* om., ib. 45 *I* om., II. 3. 50 *unlandish*
f. *uplandish*, III. 1. 68 *make* f. *made*, III. 4. 69 *the* f. *a*, ib. 106 *an* f.
and etc. (E, therefore, is of little or no value for the reestablishment $\times$
of the text.) Only for completeness' sake let us add that II. 1. 46,
47 have been first divided, and that III. 4. 152 *master* (f. *mistris*)
has been first introduced by the edition of 1657.

The old play was made accessible to modern readers by 'The
Shoemaker's Holiday, or the Gentle Craft. Nach einem Drucke
aus dem Jahre 1618 neu herausgegeben von Hermann Fritsche,
Lehrer am Gymnasium zu Thorn. Thorn 1862.' Mr. Fritsche's
edition is based on the copy of C which is preserved at the municipal library of Dantzic. The editor divided the play into fifteen
scenes, and added the *Dramatis Personæ* and numerous stage
-directions; he modernised the spelling and regulated the divi-
sion of the lines as well as the punctuation; lastly he corrected a
number of mistakes, exhibited by C. He thus hit the original
readings (AB) II. 3. 126, III. 4. 129, IV. 4. 45, V. 4. 45. In other
passages where the reading of all edd. seems to be corrupt,
Mr. Fritsche's proposals deserve to be noted, cp. III. 2. 23 and
particularly V. 5. 91. On the whole, however, Mr. Fritsche's edition
does not satisfy a philological reader, and it is hardly to be
regretted that it is now quite out of print.

Another modern edition of the play was published in Dekker's
Dramatic Works, London, Pearson, 1873, vol. I, S. 1—79. The
play is preceded by an Introductory Notice to the following effect:

There are three later editions of the Shoemakers' Holiday published
in Dekker's lifetime, bearing date 1610, 1618, and 1631 respec-
tively. The present text has been formed by a careful collation
of these with the first edition. Some of the verbal differences are
indicated in footnotes.' The text of the play, however, by no
means answers the Introductory Notice. The basis of it is the
edition of 1600; A has, it seems, merely been collated with D.
But not only have the evident mistakes of A been corrected
by means of D (I. 1. 177 *not* add., II. 1. 26 *a* add., II. 2. 11
baseness f. *bareness*, III. 1. 140 *aboord* f. *abroad*, III. 2. 2 *eighteenth* f. *eighteen*, III. 4. 1 *O Firke* add.), but a number of
inferior readings of D have without any reason been substituted
for those of A.' Cp. First Three-men's-song 13 *Forest* f. *Forests*,
I. 1. 142 *on* om., ib. 193 *come* add., II. 1. 60 *and* add., II. 2. 21 *at*
f. *in*, II. 3. 62 *Afore* f. *Fore*, II. 5. 17 *Zounds* f. *wounds*, III. 3. 94
Lurk f. *Lurch*, III. 4. 46 *time that I* f. *time I*, IV. 1. 50 *do* f. *loue*,
ib. 88 *not* om., IV. 2. 12 *Effreys* f. *Jeffres*, IV. 5. 42 *as you are
Lord Mayor* f. *as Gods in Heaven* etc. The *Varia Lectio* is scanty
in the highest degree, only seven readings being pointed out in
it. On the other hand, we find in the text more than one mistake
not to be met with in any of the old editions. Cp. I. 1. 230 *flops*
f. *slops*, II. 5. 63 *with* f. *to*, III. 1. 7 *de* om., IV. 4. 30 *sute* f. *dute*,
V. 1. 16 *loaded* f. *loaden*, V. 4. 59 *I shall* f. *shall I*. The same
arbitrary method is seen in the spelling. For the most part the
editor sticks to A; in several instances, however, he prefers D, and
not unfrequently he substitutes some spelling of his own for that
of the old edd. The punctuation, the surest criterion of a careful
edition, has been quite neglected. Moreover, not even an attempt
has been made to illustrate the contents of the play or to expound
the meaning of obsolete words and obscure expressions. After
all this, there can be no doubt that Mr. Pearson's edition cannot
stand the test to which we are used to submit a good edition of
an author either ancient or modern.

By an error easily to be accounted for, Barton Holiday (b. 1593)
was formerly thought to have been the author of the Shoemakers'
Holiday.[1]) From Henslowe's Diary, however, it appears that the

---

[1]) See Biographia Britannica, ed. Baker, Reade, Jones, London 1812,
III, p. 268 'This play has been attributed to Dr. Barton Holiday.' Vol. I,
p. 180 'The Gentle Craft' is enumerated among the plays of Thomas Dekker.

play must be attributed to Thomas Dekker. The passage in question is:[1] 'Lent unto Samewell Rowley and Thomas Dowton, the 15 of Julye, 1599, to bye a Boocke of Thomas Dickers, called the gentle Craft, the some of III s.'[2] From this entry we learn that Thomas Dekker wrote our comedy in 1599, and that, therefore, the edition of 1600 is to be considered as the second Edition of the play. The Shoemakers' Holiday is the earliest of Dekker's comedies handed down to us; for though, according to Henslowe, Dekker commenced writing for the stage as early as 1596, yet no play anterior to ours seems to have been printed or preserved.

Besides Thomas Dekker, Robert Wilson the actor seems to have had a hand in the composition of the play. This hypothesis was first started in an interesting article, entitled 'The Players who acted in The Shoemakers Holiday 1600, a Comedy by Thomas Dekker and Robert Wilson.'[3] As the question is rather an important one, it seems best to reproduce the article *in extenso.* 'My reason', the unknown writer says, 'for stating that Robert Wilson as well as Thomas Dekker was engaged upon "The Shoemakers Holiday" is that a friend of mine has a copy with the names of the two dramatists at the end of the preliminary address. The early owner of the copy, learning in some way that it had been written by Dekker and Wilson, wrote their names at the end of the above dedication if such it may be called. These names are not printed, but they have been added in manuscript moreover with the names of the actors against all the principal parts, as they were sustained when the comedy was first brought out. These are not made to precede the play in a regular list of the *Dramatis Personæ*, but they are inserted in the margin as the piece proceeds, and as the different performers enter.' The names of the actors are given as follows: Jones (King of England), H. Jeffes (Nobleman), Shawe (Lord Mayor), Massy (Rowland Lacy), Dowton (Simon Eyre), Singer (Hodge), Wilson (Firke), Jewby (Rafe), Towne (Ham-

<hr />

[1] Cp. Pearson's edition of Dekker's Works, p. XII.

[2] On the fly-leaf of his copy of the edition of 1618 Malone made the following statement: 'This play was written by Th. Dekker, and first appeared in June 1599. Hence it is that Dekker is introduced in Jonson's Poetaster under the name of Crispinus.'

[3] Papers of the Shakespeare Society, 1849, p. 110 seqq.

mond), Flower (Warner), Price (Scott), A. Jeffes (Askew), Jones
(Dodger), Day (Lovell), Birde (Dame Eyre), H. Jeffes (Jane), Dowton's
boy Ned (Rose), Alleine (Sibill). From Henslowe's Diary[1]) we
learn that these very same players were the leading actors of Nottingham's troop. 'There is nothing, however', our author continues,
'in Henslowe's Diary to establish that Wilson was an actor as well
as an author: on p. 163 he is introduced as a partner with Drayton
and Hathway in the composition of a play called 'Owen Tudor',
and in two other places (p. 157, 178) he is stated to have been
aided by the old manager with the loan of sums of money.
Nevertheless, we know, on unquestionable evidence, that he was
an actor of considerable standing, as well as an author; he was
selected as one of the Queen's Players in 1583, on account of
his 'quick, delicate, refined, extemporal wit', and Francis Meres
celebrated him for the same qualities in 1598 . . . In this play
(Shoemakers Holiday) we may presume that he contributed much
of the broad fun; and we see that he acted the part of Firke,
one of the merry jovial journeymen shoemakers of old Eyre, the
hero. Therefore, although nothing is said by Henslowe to establish
that Wilson was one of the actors in, as well as a writer for, his
company, there can be no dispute as to the fact . . . Wilson
had a very merry, rattling character in Firke, and we need enter-
tain little doubt that he wrote it himself, and for himself, with
abundant latitude for his extemporizing power.' It is much to be
regretted that the writer of the article did not choose either to
give his own or his friend's name. Notwithstanding, his whole
reasoning is not unworthy of belief. The original owner of the
book was evidently well acquainted both with our play and with
the stage of his time; knowing the actors, he may also be supposed to have been exactly informed as to the authors of the
play. It does not matter much to know whether and when Wilson
was a member of Nottingham's troop: certain it is that he was
an actor as well as an author.[2]) Thus it seems probable to us that
part of the play, and particularly its comical scenes, were written
by Robert Wilson. In England, the hypothesis as to Dekker's and

---

[1]) Page 172, 10 July 1600.

[2]) As for Wilson and his position in the dramatic literature of the
Elizabethan era, see the essay on 'The three Lords and three Ladies of
London' by Dr. Hans Fernow, Hamburg 1885.

Wilson's partnership seems to have been adopted. In an article on Mr. Fritsche's edition [1]) we read: 'On this side of the Channel we are aware that the piece was written by Thomas Dekker and Robert Wilson.'

The principal character of the play, Simon Eyre, is taken from history. In Stow's Survey of London, 1599, and in Maitland's History and Survey of London, 1756, we find the following statements. Simon (Sim, Simkin) Eyre (Eyer), from Brandon in Suffolk, an upholsterer and afterwards a draper, built Leadenhall in 1419,[2]) became a sheriff of London in 1434,[3]) was elected Lord Mayor in 1445,[4]) and finally died in 1459.[5]) About Sim Eyre's life before 1419 we have not been able to make out anything.[6]) It may

---

[1]) Athenæum, N. 1837, June 10, 1863.

[2]) Maitland, II. p. 187: 'A. D. 1419. This year Sir (?) Symon Eyre built Leadenhall, at his proper expence, as it now appears, and gave the same to the City to be employed as a publick Granary for laying up Corn against a time of Scarcity ... In this Hall was afterwards kept the Common Beam for weighing of wool, and a publick market for many foreign Commodities ..., but at present, it is converted into Warehouses, and the Area thereof unto a Meat and Leather market.' See, besides, Note ad V. 5. 134.

[3]) Stow, ed. William J. Thoms, London 1876, p. 192: 1434 Thomas Barnewell — Simon Eyre, Sheriffes; Maior, Sir Roger Oteley, Grocer, sonne to William Oteley, of Offord in Suffolke.

[4]) Stow, l. c.: 1445 Maior: Sir Simon Eyre, Draper, sonne to John Eyre, of Brandon in Suffolke.

[5]) Stow, p. 58: Within the said church [cp. ad V. 5. 134], on the north wall, was written, *Honorandus famosus mercator Simon Eyre huius operis* etc. In English thus: — "The honourable and famous merchant, Simon Eyre, founder of this work, once mayor of this city, citizen and draper of the same, departed out of this life, the 18th day of September, the year from the Incarnation of Christ 1459, and the 38th year of the reign of King Henry VI." He was buried in the parish church of St. Mary Woolnoth, in Lombard street.

[6]) In the 'Curious Account of the Origin, Rise and Death of Sir Simon Eyre, Kt, Shoe-Maker, who successively filled the dignified Offices of Sheriff and Lord Mayor of London, and built Leadenhall. Carefully revised from the original Edition. Printed and published by A. Neil, 448 Strand' Eyre's life is related in the same manner as in the play; but there can be little doubt that the Curious Account is based on Dekker's comedy. This prose -tract seems to have been the source of a burlesque poem, entitled 'The Snob's Glory, or, The Blessings of Industry. Exemplified in a short History; gratefully addressed to the Cordwainers' Company, for their generous offer of the freedom thereof, to John, Earl of Rochester. Published by Willie Smith, Who lives in Auld Reekie, 1825.'

well be that long after Eyre's death the builder of Leadenhall was supposed to have been a shoemaker himself, merely because Leadenhall was used as a leather-market. That tradition was rejected by the chronicler; but it was taken up by the poet, who formed out of it one of the most popular comedies of the age.

In the Shoemakers' Holiday, as in most plays of the Elizabethan stage, two or three stories are intertwined with each other. The author of the play has not succeeded in working those different threads into one solid and well-proportioned texture. The different elements are but loosely connected with each other; the relation of the secondary intrigues to the principal one is quite exterior. Neither has the poet tried to give any internal motives for the development of the plot or the characters of the play. Dekker was poor; like most of the contemporary playwrights, he was working for his daily bread. All his works bear the stamp of great hurry and precipitation. He had no time to fix the characters which he beheld with the clear eye of a poet, into the frame of a well-set and symmetrical plot. He therefore cannot claim a place among the first play-writers of the time. That, however, he was not destitute of poetical talent, is sufficiently testified by our play. Most of the characters with which the reader becomes acquainted in the Shoemakers' Holiday, have with apparent faithfulness been drawn from nature. There can hardly be imagined a better representative of the London tradesmen in the time of good Queen Bess than the hero of our play, Sim Eyre. Such indeed were the manners and the speech of a gay London citizen, before the rude hand of puritanism put a stop to all mirth and merriment. A worthy counterpart of Sim Eyre is Maggy, his wife. Whether we see her at home scolding at her husband and his tippling journeymen, or as Mrs. Shrieve, quite beside herself with joy and intent only upon manifesting her new dignity by a French hood and a periwig, or lastly as Lady Maioress, warmly espousing the interest of poor Miss Rose — always she appears to us as the clever portrait of a tradesman's wife. Likewise the contrast between the three journeymen is well set forth. 'Melancholy' Hodge, funny Firke, honest Rafe, all these 'mad Cappadocians' are worthy inmates of Eyre's shop. With manifest predilection the character of Jane has been treated by the poet. Even externally, by the use of verse, he indicates Jane to be different from, and superior to, all around her. The scenes where she takes leave from Rafe and gets the news of his pretended death, are among the best of the play, and must have made a deep impression on the public for which the play was intended. Quite misconceived, on the other hand, is the character of Jane's lover, Hammon: from the first to the last the part he plays is a very sad and contemptible one. Nor can we sympathize with Rose's sweetheart, Rowland Lacy. We hardly can think well of a man who so grossly neglects his duty, who so recklessly postpones the dearest interests of his country to a petty love-affair. And how unmanly and irresolute he is when fearing to be discovered by his uncle and the Lord Mayor! How slow and anxious to take the last decisive step! No, to be sure, 'pretty Rose' would have deserved to get a more steadfast and right-minded husband. Rose herself is a most charming figure. Blooming in youth and beauty, quick-witted and judicious, truly attached to the man of her choice, she even now captivates the heart of the reader. Finally, it may be added that the poet has very skilfully contrasted Lincolne, the haughty nobleman, and Oteley, the proud citizen, whose stubbornness cannot be broken but by the command of the king himself.

Well acquainted with the taste of his contemporaries, the poet thought it necessary to season the play by some 'merry three-men's-songs' and a morris-dance, and above all by burlesque or sometimes even obscene language. The indecent expressions of Firke, the equivocal discourses of Sibil, and the comical dialect of Hans must have added in a large measure to the popularity of the play.

As to the Dutch dialect spoken by Hans, it would be of no use to localize it. There seems to be no doubt that the poet did not attempt to avail himself of any particular dialect; the effect which he intended, was much easier to be attained by a few quaint words and expressions which it was not difficult to gather from the mouths of Low-German shippers and tradesmen in London.[1])

---

[1]) The play-going public of Queen Elizabeth's time liked very much to hear from the stage either English dialects or foreign idioms mixed up

The Shoemakers' Holiday may be considered as the type of the lower comedy as it was in vogue towards the end of the reign of Queen Elizabeth. It offers to the antiquarian a curious insight into the manners as well as the language of the London tradespeople of the age. For these reasons it seemed well worth while to draw the attention of friends of the Elizabethan drama to the old play, which certainly does not deserve the oblivion in which it has been buried for nearly three centuries.

———

with scraps of their mother-tongue. The greatest favourite was 'Dutch Hance', a type that recurs in several plays of the time. There is 'Hance' in 'Like will to Like', there are the two personages of the same name in Webster's Northward Ho!' and 'Westward Ho!'; there is the 'Dutch Boy' and his Master in Middleton's 'No Wit, no Help like a Woman's'; and, finally, we may mention the 'Dutch princess Hedewick' in Chapman's 'Alphonsus'. For further particulars the reader is referred to Emil Panning's essay on 'Dialektisches Englisch in Elisabethanischen Dramen' (Halle, 1884), p. 2 seqq.

———

CORRECTIONS.

I.   1. 132 (note) read *CDE* for *CD*.
III. 5. 27, 28 (note) read *prose* for *pross*.

———

THE SHOEMAKERS' HOLIDAY;

OR

THE GENTLE CRAFT.

DRAMATIS PERSONÆ.*)

THE KING.

THE EARL OF CORNWALL.

SIR HUGH LACY, *Earl of Lincoln.*

ROWLAND LACY } *his nephews.*
ASKEW

SIR ROGER OATELEY, *Lord Mayor of London.*

MR. HAMMON }
MR. WARNER } *Citizens of London.*
MR. SCOTT }

SIMON EYRE, *the Shoemaker.*

ROGER }
FIRK } *Eyre's Journeymen.*
RAFE }

LOVELL, *a Courtier.*

DODGER, *Servant to the Earl of Lincoln.*

A DUTCH SKIPPER.

A BOY.

ROSE, *Daughter to Sir Roger.*

SIBIL, *her Maid.*

MARGERY, *Wife to Simon Eyre.*

IANE, *Wife to Rafe.*

COURTIERS, ATTENDANTS, OFFICERS, SOLDIERS, HUNTERS, SHOEMAKERS, APPRENTICES, SERVANTS.

The Scene is at LONDON *and at* OLDFORD.

*) *A* DRAMATIS PERSONÆ *was first added by Fritsche.*

TO ALL GOOD FELLOWES, PROFESSORS OF THE GENTLE CRAFT, OF WHAT DEGREE SOEUER.

Kinde Gentlemen and honest boone Companions, I present you here with a merrie-conceited Comedie, called *the
Shoomakers Holyday*, acted by my Lorde Admiralls Players this
present Christmasse before the Queenes most excellent Maiestie,
for the mirth and pleasant matter by her Highnesse graciously   5
accepted, being indeede no way offensiue. The Argument of
the play I will set downe in this Epistle: *Sir Hugh Lacie,
Earle of Lincolne*, had a yong Gentleman of his owne name,
his nere kinsman, that loued the Lorde Maiors daughter of
London; to preuent and crosse which loue, the Earle caused   10
his kinsman to be sent Coronell of a companie into France:
who resigned his place to another gentleman his friend, and
came disguised like a Dutch Shoomaker to the house of *Symon
Eyre* in Towerstreete, who serued the Maior and his houshold
with shooes: the merriments that passed in Eyres house, his   15
comming to be Maior of London, *Lacies* getting his loue, and
other accidents, with two merry Three-mens-songs. Take all
in good worth that is well intended, for nothing is purposed
but mirth; mirth lengthneth long life, which, with all other
blessings, I heartily wish you. Farewell!   20

3. *by my Lord Admirals Players on a Cristmasse time* B, *at a Cristmasse time* CDE. - 4. *Maiestie. For* Qq. — 11. *Colonell* E. - 15. *shooes.
The* Qq.   17. *with two merry Three-mens-songs* omitted in E, where
also the two songs have dropped out.

THE FIRST THREE-MANS SONG.

O the month of Maie, the merrie month of Maie,
So frolicke, so gay, and so greene, so greene, so greene!
O, and then did I unto my true loue say:
'Sweete Peg, thou shalt be my Summers Queene!

5   Now the Nightingale, the prettie Nightingale,
The sweetest singer in all the Forrests quier,
Intreates thee, sweete Peggie, to heare thy true loues tale;
Loe, yonder she sitteth, her breast against a brier.

But O, I spie the Cuckoo, the Cuckoo, the Cuckoo;
10 See where she sitteth: come away, my ioy;
Come away, I prithee: I do not like, the Cuckoo
Should sing where my Peggie and I kisse and toy.'

O the month of Maie, the merrie month of Maie,
So frolike, so gay, and so greene, so greene, so greene!
15 And then did I unto my true loue say:
'Sweete Peg, thou shalt be my Summers Queene!'

THE SECOND THREE-MANS SONG.

This is to be sung at the latter end.

Cold's the wind, and wet's the raine,
    Saint Hugh be our good speede:
Ill is the weather that bringeth no gaine,
    Nor helpes good hearts in neede.

6. *Forest* D.

Trowle the boll, the iolly Nut-browne boll,   5
    And here, kind mate, to thee:
Let's sing a dirge for Saint Hughes soule,
    And downe it merrily.

Downe a downe, hey downe a downe, *(Close with the tenor boy)*
    Hey derie derie, down a down!   10
Ho, well done; to me let come!
    Ring, compasse gentle ioy.

Trowle the boll, the Nut-browne boll,
    And here, kind *etc. [as often as there be men to drinke.*
            [At last when all haue drunke, this verse:
Cold's the wind, and wet's the raine,   15
    Saint Hugh be our good speede:
Ill is the weather that bringeth no gaine,
    Nor helpes good hearts in neede.

    5. *bowle* D. — 13. *bowle* D.

THE PROLOGUE

As wretches in a storme (expecting day),
With trembling hands and eyes cast up to heauen,
Make prayers the anchor of their conquerd hopes,
So we, deere goddesse, wonder of all eyes,
5   Your meanest vassals, through mistrust and feare
To sincke into the bottome of disgrace
By our imperfit pastimes, prostrate thus
On bended knees, our sailes of hope do strike,
Dreading the bitter stormes of your dislike.
10   Since then, unhappy men, our hap is such,
That to our selves our selves no help can bring,
But needes must perish, if your saint-like cares
(Locking the temple where all mercy sits)
Refuse the tribute of our begging tongues:
15   Oh graunt, bright mirror of true chastitie,
From those life-breathing starres, your sun-like eyes,
One gratious smile: for your celestiall breath
Must send vs life, or sentence us to death.

PROLOGUE.   7. *imperfect* BCDE. — 14. *tongues.* Qq.

A PLEASANT COMEDIE OF THE GENTLE CRAFT.

ACT I.

SCENE I.

Enter LORD MAIOR, LINCOLNE.

Lincolne. My Lord Maior, you haue sundrie times
Feasted my selfe and many courtiers more:
Seldome or neuer can we be so kind
To make requitall of your courtesie.
But leauing this, I heare my cosen Lacie   5
Is much affected to your daughter Rose.
   L. Maior. True, my good Lord, and she loues him so wel
That I mislike her boldnesse in the chace.
   Lincolne. Why, my Lord Maior, think you it then a shame,
To ioine a Lacie with an Otleys name?   10
   L. Maior. Too meane is my poore girle for his high birth;
Poore cittizens must not with courtiers wed,
Who will in silkes and gay apparrell spend
More in one yeare then I am worth, by farre:
Therefore your honour neede not doubt my girle.   15
   Lincolne. Take heede, my Lord, aduise you what you do!
A verier unthrift liues not in the world,
Then is my cosen; for Ile tel you what:
Tis now almost a yeare since he requested
To trauell countries for experience;   20
I furnisht him with coyne, billes of exchange,
Letters of credite, men to waite on him,
Solicited my friends in Italie
Well to respect him. But to see the end:

ACT I. SCENE I. [*Scene* I. *London. A street:*] Fr. — 10. *Oteley's*
E. — 13. *silks and apparel* E. — 18. *I tell* DE. — 22. *waight* C. — 24. *but
see* DE.

25 Scant had he iornied through halfe Germanie,
But all his coyne was spent, his men cast off,
His billes imbezeld, and my iolly coze,
Asham'd to shew his bankerupt presence here,
Became a shoomaker in Wittenberg,
30 A goodly science for a gentleman
Of such discent! Now iudge the rest by this:
Suppose your daughter haue a thousand pound,
Ile did consume me more in one halfe yeare;
And make him heyre to all the wealth you haue,
35 One tweluemoneth's rioting wil waste it all.
Then seeke, my Lord, some honest cittizen
To wed your daughter to.
    L. Maior.   ·   I thanke your Lordship.
(Aside) Wel, foxe, I vnderstand your subtiltie.
As for your nephew, let your lordships eie
40 But watch his actions, and you neede not feare,
For I haue sent my daughter farre enough.
And yet your cosen Rowland might do well,
Now he hath learn'd an occupation;
And yet I scorne to call him sonne in law.
45   *Lincolne.* I, but I haue a better trade for him:
I thanke his grace, he hath appointed him
Chiefe colonell of all those companies
Mustred in London and the shires about,
To serue his highnesse in those warres of France.
50 See where he comes! —

        Enter LOUELL, LACIE, *and* ASKEW.

          Louel, what newes with you?
   Louell. My Lord of Lincolne, tis his highnesse will,
That presently your cosen ship for France
With all his powers; he would not for a million,
But they should land at Deepe within foure daies.
55   *Lincolne.* Goe certifie his grace, it shall be done. [*Exit* LOUELL.

---

27. *imbezeled* E. – 29. *Wittemberge* CDE. — 33. *consume more* CDE.
— 38. *(Aside)* om. in Qq. — 39. *Jlordship's* E. — 41. *sent* om. A. — 45. *I
but*] *But* DE. — 46. *appoinied* E. — 50. The stage-direction after *you?* in
Qq. — 55. [*Exit Louell*] om. BCDE.

Now, cosen Lacie, in what forwardnesse
Are all your companies?
 Lacie.   All wel prepar'd.
The men of Hartfordshire lie at Mile-end,
Suffolke and Essex traine in Tuttle-fields,
The Londoners and those of Middlesex,   60
All gallantly prepar'd in Finsbury,
With frolike spirits long for their parting hower.
 L. Maior. They haue their imprest, coates, and furniture;
And, if it please your cosen Lacie come
To the Guild Hall, he shall receiue his pay;   65
And twentie pounds besides my brethren
Will freely giue him, to approue our loues
We beare unto my Lord, your uncle here.
 Lacie. I thanke your honour.
 Lincolne.   Thankes, my good Lord Maior.
 L. Maior. At the Guild Hal we will expect your comming. 70
              [*Exit.*

 Lincolne. To approve your loues to me? No subtiltie!
Nephew, that twentie pound he doth bestow
For ioy to rid you from his daughter Rose.
But, cosens both, now here are none but friends,
I would not haue you cast an amorous eie   75
Upon so meane a proiect as the loue
Of a gay, wanton, painted cittizen.
I know, this churle euen in the height of scorne
Doth hate the mixture of his bloud with thine.
I pray thee, do thou so! Remember, coze,   80
What honourable fortunes wayt on thee:
Increase the kings loue, which so brightly shines,
And gilds thy hopes. I haue no heire but thee, —
And yet not thee, if with a wayward spirit
Thou start from the true byas of my loue.   85
 Lacie. My Lord, I will for honor, not desire
Of land or liuings, or to be your heire,

---

56. *for wardnesse* C. — 58. *lie*] *are* CDE. — 63. *heve* E. — 66. *brethren,*
used as a trisyllable. — 71. *appove* B. — 72. *he*] *the* B. — 77. *wanted-painton* B. — 82. *Intreate* CDE. — 87. *lands* CDE.

So guide my actions in pursuit of France,
As shall adde glorie to the Lacies name.

90   *Lincolne.* Coze, for those words heres thirtie Portugues,
And, Nephew Askew, there's a few for you.
Faire Honour, in her loftiest eminence,
Staies in France for you, till you fetch her thence.
Then, nephewes, clap swift wings on your dissignes:

95   Be gone, be gone, make haste to the Guild Hall;
There presently Ile meet you. Do not stay:
Where honour beckons, shame attends delay.   [*Exit.*

    Askew. How gladly would your vncle haue you gone!
    Lacie. True, coze, but Ile ore-reach his policies.

100 I haue some serious businesse for three dayes,
Which nothing but my presence can dispatch.
You, therefore, cosen, with the companies
Shall haste to Douer; there Ile meete with you:
Or, if I stay past my prefixed time,

105 Away for France; weele meete in Normandie.
The twentie pounds my Lord Maior giues to me
You shall receiue, and these ten portugues,
Part of mine vncles thirtie. Gentle coze,
Haue care to our great charge; I know, your wisedome

110 Hath tride it selfe in higher consequence.
    Askew. Coze, al my selfe am yours: yet haue this care,
To lodge in London with all secrecie;
Our vncle Lincolne hath, besides his owne,
Many a iealous eie, that in your face

115 Stares onely to watch meanes for your disgrace.
    Lacie. Stay, cosen, who be these?

Enter SYMON EYRE, *his Wife*, HODGE, FIRK, IANE, *and* RAFE
with a peece.

    Eyre. Leaue whining, leaue whining! Away with this
whimpring, this pewling, these blubbring teares, and these wet

---

88. *pursnit* E. — 94. *nephew* CDE. — 97. *beckons*] *become* Qq. Corrected
by Malone in A and C. — 99. *pollicies* C. — 116. Om. in CDE. — 116. Stage-
direction. *Hodg* E. — 118. *puling* CDE.

eies! He get thy husband discharg'd, I warrant thee, sweete
lane; go to!   120

Hodge. Master, here be the captaines.

Eyre. Peace, Hodge; husht, ye knave, husht!

Firke. Here be the caualiers and the coronels, maister.

Eyre. Peace, Firke; peace, my fine Firke! Stand by with
your pishery-pasherie, away! I am a man of the best presence; 125
Ile speake to them, and they were Popes. — Gentlemen, captaines, colonels, commanders! Braue men, braue leaders, may
it please you to giue me audience. I am Simon Eyre, the
mad Shoomaker of Towerstreete; this wench with the mealy
mouth that wil neuer tire, is my wife, I can tel you; heres 130
Hodge, my man and my foreman; heres Firke, my fine firking
iourneyman, and this is blubbered Iane. Al we come to be
suters for this honest Rafe. Keepe him at home, and as I
am a true shoomaker and a gentleman of the Gentle Craft,
buy spurs your self, and Ile find ye bootes these seuen yeeres. 135

Wife. Seuen yeares, husband?

Eyre. Peace, Midriffe, peace! I know what I do. Peace!

Firke. Truly, master cormorant, you shal do God good
seruice to let Rafe and his wife stay together. Shees a young
new-married woman; if you take her husband away from her 140
a night, you undoo her; she may beg in the day-time; for
hees as good a workman at a pricke and an awle, as any
is in our trade.

Iane. O let him stay, else I shal be undone.

Firke. I, truly, she shal be laid at one side like a paire of 145
old shooes else, and be occupied for no use.

Lacie. Truly, my friends, it lies not in my power:
The Londoners are prest, paide, and set forth
By the Lord Maior; I cannot change a man.

Hodge. Why, then you were as good be a corporall as a 150
colonel, if you cannot discharge one good fellow; and I tell
you true, I thinke you doe more then you can answere, to
presse a man within a yeare and a day of his mariage.

121. *Maister* C. — 122. *you* CDE. — 123. *and*] *add* B; *Master* DE. —
126. *and*] *an* DE. — 130. *that wil neuer tire* om. CDE. — 132. *is*] *his* CD.
— 135. *ye*] *you* CDE. — 138. *maister* C. — 142. *an* om. DE. — 145. *a one*
DE. — 150. *Hoge* B.

Eyre. Well said, melancholy Hodge; gramercy, my fine
155 foreman.

Wife. Truly, gentlemen, it were il done for such as you,
to stand so stiffely against a poore yong wife, considering her
case, she is new-married, but let that passe: I pray, deale
not roughly with her; her husband is a yong man, and but
160 newly entred, but let that passe.

Eyre. Away with your pisherie-pasherie, your pols and
your edipolls! Peace, Midaffe; silence, Cisly Bumtrincket!
Let your head speake.

Firke. Yea, and the hornes too, master.

165 *Eyre.* Too soone, my fine Firk, too soone! Peace, scoundrels! See you this man? Captaines, you will not release
him? Wel, let him go; hee's a proper shot; let him vanish!
Peace, Iane, drie up thy teares, theile make his powder dankish.
Take him, braue men; Hector of Troy was an hackney to
170 him, Hercules and Termagant scoundrelles, Prince Arthurs
Round-table — by the Lord of Ludgate — nere fed such a
tall, such a dapper swordman; by the life of Pharo, a braue,
resolute swordman! Peace, Iane! I say no more, mad
knaues.

175 *Firk.* See, see, Hodge, how my maister raues in commen-
dation of Rafe!

Hodge. Raph, thart a gull, by this hand, and thou goest not.

Askew. I am glad, good master Ayre, it is my hap
To meete so resolute a souldiour.
180 Trust me, for your report and loue to him,
A common slight regard shall not respect him.

Lacie. Is thy name Raph?

Raph.   Yes, sir.

Lacie.   Give me thy hand;
Thou shalt not want, as I am a gentleman.
Woman, be patient; God, no doubt, wil send

154. *gramarcy* CD. — 156. *Gntlemen* C, *Gentleman* E. — 158. *newly*
DE. — 162. *edipols* CDE; *Midasse* CDE. — 167. *he is* CDE. — 169. *a
hackney* DE. — 172. *Pharoah* C, *Pharoh* DE. — 175. *master* D; *commendations* C. — 177. *thou'rt* DE; *and*] *an* D, om. E; *not* om. ABC. —
178. *maister* C.

Thy husband safe againe; but he must go,   185
His countries quarrel sayes: it shall be so.

Hodge. Thart a gull, by my stirrop, if thou doest not goe.
I will not haue thee strike thy gimblet into these weake vessels;
pricke thine enemies, Rafe.

Enter DODGER.

Dodger. My Lord, your vncle on the Tower-hill   190
Stayes with the Lord Mayor and the Aldermen,
And doth request you with all speede you may,
To hasten thither.

Askew.   Cosin, lets go.

Lacy. Dodger, runne you before, tel them we come. —
This Dodger is mine vncles parasite,   [*Exit* DODGER. 195
The arrantst varlet that e're breathd on earth;
⌐He sets more discord in a noble house ⌐
By one daies broching of his pickethanke tales,
Than can be salu'd againe in twentie yeares,
And he, I feare, shall go with vs to France,   200
To prie into our actions.

Askew.   Therefore, coze,
It shall behooue you to be circumspect.

Lacy. Feare not, good cosen. — Raph, hie to your colours.

Raph. I must, because theres no remedie;
But, gentle maister and my louing dame,   205
As you haue alwaies beene a friend to me,
So in mine absence thinke upon my wife.

Iane. Alas, my Raph.

Wife. She cannot speake for weeping.

Eyre. Peace, you crackt groates, you mustard tokens, dis- 210
quiet not the braue souldier. Goe thy waies, Raph!

Iane. I, I, you bid him go; what shal I do,
When he is gone?

186. *it must* CDE. — 187. *Thou'rt* DE. — 188. *gimlet* CDE. —
191. *Stayey* E. -- 193. *lets* = let us; *Cousin, come, lets go* B, *Cousin, come,
let us go* CDE. — 195. *my* DE. — 196. *arrants* B, *arranst* DE. — 197. *in*]
of BC. — 198. *broaching* DE; *of*] *in* BCDE; *pick-hanke* E. — 204. *there
is* BCDE.   205. *master* D. --- 207. *mine*] *my* BCDE.   212—213. One
line in Qq.

    Firk. Why, be doing with me or my fellow Hodge; be
215 not idle.

    Eyre. Let me see thy hand, Iane. This fine hand, this
white hand, these prettie fingers must spin, must card, must
worke; worke, you bombast-cotten-candle-queane, worke
for your liuing, with a pox to you. — Hold thee, Raph,
220 heres fiue sixpences for thee; fight for the honour of the
Gentle Craft, for the Gentlemen Shoomakers, the couragious Cordwainers, the flower of S. Martins, the mad knaues
of Bedlem, Fleetstreete, Towerstreete and Whitechappell; cracke
me the crownes of the French knaues; a poxe on them, cracke
225 them; fight, by the Lord of Ludgate; fight, my fine boy!

    Firke. Here, Rafe, heres' three twopences: two carry into
France, the third shal wash our soules at parting, for sorrow
is drie. For my sake, firke the *Basa mon cues.*

    Hodge. Raph, I am heauy at parting; but heres a shilling
230 for thee. God send thee to cramme thy slops with French
crownes, and thy enemies bellies with bullets.

    Raph. I thanke you, maister, and I thanke you all.
Now, gentle wife, my louing louely Iane, ·
Rich men, at parting, giue their wiues rich gifts,
235 Iewels and rings, to grace their lillie hands.
Thou know'st our trade makes rings for womens heeles:
Here take this paire of shooes, cut out by Hodge,
Sticht by my fellow Firke, seam'd by my selfe,
Made up and pinckt with letters for thy name.
240 Weare them, my deere Iane, for thy husbands sake;
And euerie morning, when thou pull'st them on,
Remember me, and pray for my returne.
Make much of them; for I haue made them so,
That I can know them from a thousand mo.

Sound drumme. Enter LORD MAIOR, LINCOLNE, LACY, ASKEW,
DODGER, *and souldiers. They passe ouer the stage;* RAFE *falles in
amongest them;* FIRKE *and the rest cry farewel etc., and so exeunt.*

---

    218. *bumbast* CDE; *bombast cotten-candle-queane* ABC. — 223. *Bed-
lam* F. — 226. *two twopences, to carry* CDE. — 228. *fike* B. — 232. *ye
master* DE.   233. *louing* om. F.

ACT II.

SCENE I.

Enter ROSE, *alone, making a Garland.*

Rose.   Here sit thou downe upon this flowry banke,
And make a garland for thy Lacies head.
These pinkes, these roses, and these violets,
These blushing gillillowers, these marigoldes,
The faire embrodery of his coronet,   5
Carry not halfe such beauty in their cheekes,
As the sweete countnaunce of my Lacy doth.
O my most unkinde father! O my starres,
Why lowrde you so at my natiuity,
To make me loue, yet liue, robd of my loue?   10
Here as a theefe am I imprisoned
For my deere Lacies sake within those walles,
Which by my fathers cost were builded up
For better purposes; here must I languish
For him that doth as much lament, I know,   15
Mine absence, as for him I pine in woe.

Enter SIBIL.

Sibil.   Good morrow, yong Mistris. I am sure you make
that garland for me; against *I shall be Lady of the Haruest.*
Rose.   Sibil, what news at London?
Sibil.   None but good; my Lord Mayor, your father, and   20
maister Philpot, your uncle, and maister Scot, your coosin,
and mistris Frigbottom by Doctors Commons, doe all, by my
troth, send you most hearty commendations.
Rose.   Did Lacy send kind greetings to his loue?
Sibil.   O yes, out of cry, by my troth. I scant knew him;   25
here a wore a scarffe, and here a scarfe, here a bunch of
fethers, and here pretious stones and iewells, and a paire of
garters, — O, monstrous! like one of our yellow silke curtains

---

ACT II. SCENE I. [*Scene 2. Oldford. A garden.*] Fr. — 5. *embroy-
dery* C.   21. *master* D. — 22. *Doctor* C. — 26. *wore scarffe* AB; *scarf*
CDE.

at home here in Old-ford house, here in maister Belly-mounts
30 chamber. I stoode at our doore in Cornehill, lookt at him,
he at me indeed, spake to him, but he not to me, not a
word; mary gup, thought I, with a wanion! He passt by me
as prowde - - Mary foh! are you growne humorous, thought
I; and so shut the doore, and in I came.

35 *Rose.* O Sibill, how dost thou my Lacy wrong!
My Rowland is as gentle as a lambe,
No doue was euer halfe so milde as he.

Sibil. Milde? yea, as a bushel of stampt crabs. He lookt
upon me as sowre as veriuice. Goe thy wayes, thought I;
40 thou maist be much in my gaskins, but nothing in my neather-
stockes. This is your fault, mistris, to loue him that loues
not you; he thinkes scorne to do as he's done to; but if I
were as you, Ide cry: *go by, Ieronimo, go by!*

Ide set mine olde debts against my new driblets,
45 *And the hares foot against the goose giblets,*
For if euer I sigh, when sleepe I shoulde take,
Pray God, I may loose my mayden-head when I wake.

Rose. Will my loue leaue me then, and go to France?

Sibil. I knowe not that, but I am sure I see him stalke
50 before the souldiers. By my troth, he is a propper man;
but he is proper that proper doth. Let him goe snicke-up
yong mistris.

Rose. Get thee to London, and learne perfectly,
Whether my Lacy go to France, or no.
55 Do this, and I wil giue thee for thy paines
My cambricke apron and my romish gloues,
My purple stockings and a stomacher.
Say, wilt thou do this, Sibil, for my sake?

Sibil. Wil I, quoth a? At whose suit? By my troth, yes
60 Ile go. A cambricke apron, gloues, a paire of purple stockings,
and a stomacher! Ile sweat in purple, mistris, for you; ile
take any thing that comes a Gods name. O rich! a cambricke

---

29. *master* D. — 31. *speak* E; *he to me* CDE. — 32. *gip* CDE. —
37. *euer* om. E. — 38. *stamgt* F. — 44—45. Printed as prose in Qq. —
44. *my olde* DE. — 46—47. Printed as prose in ABCD. — 57, 60. *stockins*
DE. 60. *and a pair* DE. — 62. *a Gods*] *in Gods* DE.

apron! Faith, then haue at 'up tailes all'. Ile go liggy
-loggy to London, and be here in a trice, yong mistris. [*Exit.*

   Rose. Do so, good Sibill. Meane time wretched I   65
Will sit and sigh for his lost company.   [*Exit.*

SCENE II.

Enter ROWLAND LACY, *like a Dutch Shoemaker.*

   Lacy. How many shapes haue gods and kings devisde,
Thereby to compasse their desired loues!
It is no shame for Rowland Lacy, then,
To clothe his cunning with the Gentle Craft,
That, thus disguisde, I may unknowne possesse   5
The onely happie presence of my Rose.
For her haue I forsooke my charge in France,
Incurd the kings displeasure, and stird up
Rough hatred in mine vncle Lincolnes brest.
O loue, how powerfull art thou, that canst change   10
High birth to basenesse, and a noble mind
To the meane semblance of a shooemaker!
But thus it must be. For her cruell father,
Hating the single vnion of our soules,
Has secretly conueyd my Rose from London,   15
To barre me of her presence; but I trust,
Fortune and this disguise will furder me
Once more to view her beautie, gaine her sight.
Here in Towerstreete with Ayre the shooemaker
Meane I a while to worke; I know the trade,   20
I learn't it when I was in Wittenberge.
Then cheere thy hoping sprites, be not dismaide,
Thou canst not want: do Fortune what she can,
The Gentle Craft is liuing for a man.   [*Exit.*

64. [*Exit*] om. CDE.
    SCENE II. [*Scene* 3. *London. A Street.*] Fr. — 9. *my* DE. — 11. *b. re-*
nesse ABC. — 17. *further* CDE. — 21. *learne* C; *at Wittemberge* D, *at*
Wittemberg E. — 22. *spirits* CDE.

Scene III.

Enter Eyre, *making himselfe readie.*

Eyre. Where be these boyes, these girles, these drabbes, these scoundrels? They wallow in the fat brewisse of my bountie, and licke vp the crums of my table, yet wil not rise to see my walkes cleansed. Come out, you powder-beefe
5 -queanes! What, Nan! what, Madge Mumble-crust. Come out, you fatte Midriffe-swag-belly-whores, and sweepe me these kennels that the noysome stench offende not the noses of my neighbours. What, Firke, I say; what, Hodge! Open my shop-windowes! What, Firke, I say!

Enter Firke.

10   *Firke.* O master, ist you that speake bandog and bedlam this morning? I was in a dreame, and muzed what madde man was got into the streete so earlie; haue you drunke this morning that your throate is so cleere?

Eyre. Ah, well saide, Firke; well said, Firke. To worke,
15 my fine knaue, to worke! Wash thy face, and thou't be more blest.

Firke. Let them wash my face that will eate it. Good maister, send for a sowce-wife, if youle haue my face cleaner.

Enter Hodge.

Eyre. Away, slouen! auaunt, scoundrell! — Good morrow,
20 Hodge; good morrow, my fine foreman.

Hodge. O maister, good morrow; yare an earlie stirrer. Heeres a faire morning. — Good morrow, Firke, I could haue slept this howre. Heeres a braue day towards.

Eyre. Oh, haste to worke, my fine foreman, haste to worke.
25   *Firke.* Maister, I am drie as dust to heare my fellow Roger talke of faire weather; let vs pray for good leather, and let

---

Scene III. [*Scene* 4. *An open yard before Eyre's house.*] Fr. —
4. *clensed* C. — 5. *Madge-mumble-crust* Qq. — 6. *Midriffe-swag, belly
-whores* A. — 7. *stench*] *filth* CDE; *nose* AB. — 8. *my* om. D. — 10. *maister*
C; *bang dog* B. — 15. *thou'lt* CD. — 18. *master* D; *souse-wife* CDE; *you
will* BCDE. — 21, 25. *master* D. — 23. *toward* C.

clownes and plowboyes and those that worke in the fieldes
pray for braue dayes. Wee worke in a drie shop; what care
I if it raine?

Enter EYRE'S WIFE.

Eyre. How now, dame Margery, can you see to rise? 30
Trip and go, call up the drabs, your maides.

Wife. See to rise? I hope tis time inough, tis earlie
inough for any woman to be seene abroad. I maruaile how
manie wiues in Towerstreet are up so soon. Gods me, tis
not noone, — heres a yawling! 35

Eyre. Peace, Margerie, peace! Wheres Cisly Bumtrinket,
your maide? She has a priuie fault, she farts in her sleepe.
Call the queane up; if my men want shooethread, ile swinge
her in a stirrop.

Firke. Yet, thats but a drie beating; heres still a signe 40
of drought.

Enter LACY, *singing.*

Lacy.   *Der was een bore van Gelderland,*
            Frolick si byen;
        He was als dronck he cold nyet stand,
            l'psolce se byen. 45
        Tap eens de canneken,
        Drincke, shone mannekin.

Firke. Master, for my life, yonders a brother of the Gentle
Craft; if he beare not saint Hughes bones, Ile forfeit my
bones: hees some vplandish workman: hire him, good master, 50
that I may learne some gibble-gabble; twill make us worke
the faster.

Eyre. Peace, Firke! A hard world! Let him passe, let
him vanish; we haue iourneymen enow. Peace, my fine Firke!

Wife. Nay, nay, y'are best follow your mans councell; you 55
shal see what wil come on't: we haue not men enow, but we
must entertaine euery butter-boxe; but let that passe.

32. *I hope*] hope B. — 36. *Her's* E. — 44. *dronke* C, *drunke* DE. —
45. *up selcese byen* E. — 46. *canneken* C. — 47. *drinck* C; *shoue* A, *shene*
B, *sheue* C, *sheve* DE. — 48, 50. *Maister* C. — 50. *unlandish* DE.

Hodge. Dame, fore God, if my maister follow your counsell, heele consume little beefe. He shal be glad of men, and hee 60 can catch them.

Firke. I, that he shall.

Hodge. Fore God, a proper man, and I warrant, a fine workman. Maister, farewell; Dame, adew; if such a man as he cannot find worke, Hodge is not for you. [*Offers to goe.* 65 *Eyre.* Stay, my fine Hodge.

Firke. Faith, and your foreman goe, dame, you must take a iourney to seeke a new iorneyman; if Roger remoue, Firke followes. If S. Hughs bones shall not be set a-worke, I may pricke mine awle in the wals, and goe play. Fare ye wel, 70 master; God buy, dame.

Eyre. Tarrie, my fine Hodge, my briske foreman! Stay, Firke! Peace, pudding-broath! By the Lord of Ludgate, I loue my men as my life. Peace, you gallimafrie! Hodge, if he want worke, Ile hire him. One of you to him; stay, 75 — he comes to vs.

Lacie. Goeden dach, meester, ende v vro oak.

Firke. Nayls, if I should speake after him without drinking, 1 shuld choke. And you, frind Oake, are you of the Gentle Craft?

80 *Lacie.* Yaw, yaw, ik bin den skomawker.

Firke. Den skomaker, quoth a! And heark you, skomaker, haue you al your tooles, a good rubbing-pinne, a good stopper, a good dresser, your foure sorts of awles, and your two balles of waxe, your paring knife, your hand- and thumb-85 leathers, and good S. Hughs bones to smooth up your worke?

Lacie. Yaw, yaw; be niet vorveard. Ik hab all de dingen voour mack skooes groot and cleane.

Firke. Ha, ha! Good maister, hire him; heele make me laugh so that I shal worke more in mirth then I can in 90 earnest.

Eyre. Heare ye, friend, haue ye any skill in the mistery of Cordwainers?

58, 63. *Master* D. — 62. *Afore* CDE. — 68. *followres* B; *Hughes* C. — 73. *gallimaufrey* CDE. -- 74. *I hire* DE. — 80. *Ich beene den skoomaker* CDE. — 82. *pin* CDE. — 83. *sort* DE; *aules* CDE. — 84. *thum-leathers* DE. — 88. *master* D. — 91. *ye*] *you* CDE (twice).

Lacie. Ik weet niet wat yow seg; ich verstaw you niet.

Firke. Why, thus, man: (*imitating by gesture a shoemaker at work*) Ich verste v niet, quoth a.   95

Lacie. Yaw, yaw, yaw; ick can dat wel doen.

Firke. Yaw, yaw! He speakes yawing like a Jacke-daw that gapes to be fed with cheese-curdes. Oh, heele giue a villanous pul at a can of double-beere; but Hodge and I haue the vantage, we must drinke first, because wee are the   100 eldest iourneymen.

Eyre. What is thy name?

Lacie. Hans — Hans Meulter.

Eyre. Giue me thy hand; th'art welcome. — Hodge, entertaine him; Fyrk, bid him welcome; come, Hans. Runne, wife,   105 bid your maids, your trullibubs, make readie my fine mens breakefasts. To him, Hodge!

Hodge. Hans, th'art welcome; use thy selfe friendly, for we are good fellowes; if not, thou shalt be fought with, wert thou bigger then a giant.   110

Fyrk. Yea, and drunke with, wert thou Gargantua. My maister keepes no cowards, I tell thee. — Hoe, boy, bring him an heele-blocke, heers a new iourneyman. [*Enter Boy.*]

Lacy. O, ich wersto you; ich moet een halue dossen cans betaelen; here, boy, nempt dis skilling, tap eens freelicke.   115
[*Exit Boy.*]

Eyre. Quicke, snipper-snapper, away! Fyrk, scowre thy throate, thou shalt wash it with Castilian licour. [*Enter Boy.*] Come, my last of the fiues, giue me a can. Have to thee, Hans; here, Hodge; here, Fyrk; drinke, you mad Greeks, and worke like true Troians, and pray for Simon Eyre, the   120 shoomaker. — Here, Hans, and th'art welcome.

Fyrk. Lo, dame, you would haue lost a good fellow that wil teach us to laugh. This beer came hopping in well.

Wife. Simon, it is almost seuen.

Eyre. Is't so, dame Clapper-dudgeon? Is't seuen a clocke,   125 and my mens breakefast not readie? Trip and goe, you

---

93. *Ick weet* C; *you seg* C; *vestaw* A. — 94. (*Imitating ... work*) added by Fr. — 97. *yawning* DE. — 104. *thou art* CDE. — 112. *master* D. — 115. *betalen* CDE; *here*] *nere* DE; *oens* D, *ones* E. — 120. *Troyans* CD. — 126. *breakfasts* C.

sowst cunger, away! Come, you madde Hiperboreans; follow
me, Hodge; follow me, Hans; come after, my fine Fyrk; to
worke, to worke a while, and then to breakfast!   [*Exit.*

130   *Fyrk.*   Soft! Yaw, yaw, good Hans, though my master
haue no more wit but to call you afore mee, I am not so
foolish to go behind you, I being the elder iourneyman.

[*Exeunt.*

SCENE IV.

[*Hollowing within*] *Enter* WARNER *and* HAMMON, *like Hunters.*

Hammon.   Cosen, beate euery brake, the game's not farre,
This way with winged feete he fled from death,
Whilst the pursuing hounds, senting his steps,
Find out his high-way to destruction.
5   Besides, the millers boy told me euen now,
He saw him take soile, and he hallowed him,
Affirming him to have been so embost
That long he could not hold.
Warner.   If it be so,
Tis best we trace these meddowes by Old-Ford.

[*A noise of Hunters within; Enter a Boy.*]

10   *Hammon.*   How now, boy? Wheres the deere? speak,
                                        sawst thou him?
Boy.   O yea; I saw him leape through a hedge, and then
ouer a ditch, then at my Lord Maiors pale, ouer he skipt me,
and in he went me, and 'holla' the hunters cride, and
'there, boy; there, boy!' But there he is, a mine honestie.
15   *Hammon.*   Boy, God amercy. Cosen, lets away;
I hope we shal find better sport to-day.   [*Exeunt.*

SCENE V.

[*Hunting within*] *Enter* ROSE *and* SIBILL.

Rose.   Why, Sibill, wilt thou proue a forrester?
Sibill.   Upon some no; forrester, go by; no, faith, mistris.
The deere came running into the barne through the orchard

---

127. *Hiperborians* E. — 130. *maister* C.

SCENE IV. (*Scene 5. A field near Oldford.*) Fr. — Stage-dir. *Holo-
wing* C. — 6. *saile* A, *soil* BDE, *soyle* C; *hollowed* DE. — 7. *him so
embost* Qq. — 16. *we*] *I* CDE.

and ouer the pale; I wot wel, I lookt as pale as a new cheese
to see him. But whip, saies good man Pinne-close, vp with 5
his flaile, and our Nicke with a prong, and downe he fell,
and they upon him, and I upon them. By my troth, we had
such sport; and in the end we ended him; his throate we
cut, flead him, unhornd him, and my Lord Maior shal eat of
him anon, when he comes.   [*Horns sound within.* 10
    Rose. Heark, heark, the hunters come; y'are best take heed,
Theyle haue a saying to you for this deede.

          Enter HAMMON, WARNER, *Huntsmen, and Boy.*
Hammon. God saue you, faire ladies.
Sibill.   Ladies, o grosse!
Warner. Came not a bucke this way?
Rose.   No, but two does.
Hammon. And which way went they? Faith, weel hunt at those. 15
Sibill. At those? upon some no: when, can you tell?
Warner. Upon some I.
Sibill.   Good Lord!
Warner.   Wounds! Then farewell!
Hammon. Boy, which way went he?
Boy.   This way, sir, he ranne.
Hammon. This way he ranne indeede, faire mistris Rose;
Our game was lately in your orchard seene.   20
Warner. Can you aduise, which way he tooke his flight?
Sibill. Followe your nose; his hornes will guide you right.
Warner. Thart a mad wench.
Sibill.   O, rich!
Rose.   Trust me, not I.
It is not like that the wild forrest-deere
Would come so neare to places of resort;   25
You are deceiu'd, he fled some other way.
Warner. Which way, my suger-candie, can you shew?
Sibill. Come up, good honnisops, vpon some no.
Rose. Why doe you stay, and not pursue your game?

    SCENE V. [*Scene 6. Another part of the field.*] Fr. — 5. *pinne-close* A,
Pinclose CDE. — 7. *uppon* C. — 9. *unhorned* DE. — 10. Stage-dir. *Horner*
BC. — 11, 12. Printed as prose in B. — 17. *Zounds* DE. — 24. *that* om. A.
— 28. *honisops* DE.

30   *Sibill.* Ile hold my life, their hunting-nags be lame.
      Hammon. A deere more deere is found within this place.
      Rose. But not the deere, sir, which you had in chace.
      Hammon. I chac'd the deere, but this deere chaceth me.
      Rose. The strangest hunting that euer I see.
35   But wheres your parke?   [*She offers to goe away.*
      Hammon.   Tis here: O stay!
      Rose. Impale me, and then I will not stray.
      Warner. They wrangle, wench; we are more kind then they.
      Sibill. What kind of hart is that deere hart, you seeke?
      Warner. A hart, deare hart.
      Sibil.   Who euer saw the like?
40   *Rose.* To lose your heart, is't possible you can?
      Hammon. My heart is lost.
      Rose.   Alacke, good gentleman!
      Hammon. This poore lost hart would I wish you might find.
      Rose. You, by such lucke, might proue your hart a hind.
      Hammon. Why, Lucke had hornes, so haue I heard some say.
45   *Rose.* Now, God, and't be his wil, send Luck into your way.

              Enter L. MAIOR *and Seruants.*

      L. Maior. What, M. Hammon? Welcome to Old-Ford!
      Sibill. Gods pittikins, hands off, sir! Heers my Lord.
      L. Maior. I heare you had ill lucke, and lost your game.
      Hammon. Tis true, my Lord.
      L. Maior.   I am sorie for the same.
50   What gentleman is this?
      Hammon.   My brother-in-law.
      L. Maior. Y'are welcome both; sith Fortune offers you
      Into my hands, you shal not part from hence,
      Until you haue refresht your wearied limmes.
      Go, Sibel, couer the boord! You shal be guest
55   To no good cheare, but euen a hunters feast.
      Hammon. I thanke your Lordship. — Cosen, on my life,
      For our lost venison I shal find a wife.   [*Exeunt.*
      L. Maior. In, gentlemen; Ile not be absent long. —
      This Hammon is a proper gentleman,

      32. *chase* C. — 33. *chaseth* C. — 36. *Impale,* used as a trisyllable. —
38. *that, deere* A. — 54. *Sibell* C.

A citizen by birth, fairely allide;   60
How fit an husband were he for my girle!
Wel, I wil in, and do the best I can,
To match my daughter to this gentleman.   [*Exit.*

ACT III.

SCENE I.

Enter LACIE, SKIPPER, HODGE, *and* FIRKE.

Skipper. Ick sal yow wat seggen, Hans; dis skip, dat comen
from Candy, is al vol, by gots sacrament, van sugar, ciuet,
almonds, cambrick, end alle dingen, towsand towsand ding.
Nempt it, Hans, nempt it vor v meester. Daer be de bils
van laden. Your meester Simon Eyre sal hae good copen. 5
Wat seggen yow, Hans?

Firk. Wat seggen de reggen de copen, slopen — laugh,
Hodge, laugh!

Lacie. Mine lieuer broder Firk, bringt meester Eyre tot det
signe vn swannekin; daer sal yow finde dis skipper end 10
me. Wat seggen yow, broder Firk? Doot it, Hodge. Come,
skipper.   [*Exeunt.*

Firk. Bring him, quod you? Heers no knauerie, to bring
my master to buy a ship, worth the lading of 2 or 3 hundred
thousand pounds. Alas, thats nothing; a trifle, a bable, Hodge. 15

Hodge. The truth is, Firk, that the marchant owner of the
ship dares not shew his head, and therefore this skipper that
deales for him, for the loue he beares to Hans, offers my
master Eyre a bargaine in the commodities. He shal haue a
reasonable day of payment; he may sel the wares by that 20
time, and be an huge gainer himselfe.

Firk. Yea, but can my fellow Hans lend my master
twentie porpentines as an earnest pennie?

Hodge. Portegues, thou wouldst say; here they be, Firke;
heark, they gingle in my pocket like S. Mary Overies bels. 25

61 *a husband* DE.
ACT III. SCENE I. [*Scene 7. A room in Eyre's house.*] FT. — 1. *Ich*
E; *you* E. — 2. *wol* Qq. — 3. *almond* BCDE. — 4. *bills* DE. — 5. *master*
Symon D. — 9. *tot*] *lot* Qq.; *det*] *den* A. — 10. *sign* E; *swannekiu* DE;
dare CDE; *you finds* DE. — 11. *you* E. — 14. *maister* C. — 21. *be*] *he* E.
— 23. *propentines* C. — 25. *S. Mary Queries* ABC.

Enter EYRE *and his Wife.*

Firk. Mum, here comes my dame and my maister. Sheele scold, on my life, for loytering this Monday; but al's one, let them al say what they can, Monday's our holyday.

Wife. You sing, sir Sauce, but I beshrew your heart,
30   I feare, for this your singing we shal smart.

Firk. Smart for me, dame; why, dame, why?

Hodge. Maister, I hope, yowle not suffer my dame to take downe your iourneymen.

Firk. If she take me downe, Ile take her vp; yea, and
35 take her downe too, a button-hole lower.

Eyre. Peace, Firke; not I, Hodge; by the life of Pharao, by the Lord of Ludgate, by this beard, euery haire whereof I valew at a kings ransome, shee shal not meddle with you. — Peace, you bumbast-cotten-candle-queane; away, queene
40 of clubs; quarrel not with me and my men, with me and my fine Firke; Ile firke you, if you do.

Wife. Yea, yea, man, you may vse me as you please; but let that passe.

Eyre. Let it passe, let it vanish away; peace! Am I
45 not Simon Eyre? Are not these my braue men, braue shoomakers, all gentlemen of the gentle craft? Prince am I none, yet am I noblie borne, as beeing the sole sonne of a shoomaker. Away, rubbish; vanish, melt; melt like kitchin-stuffe.

50 *Wife.* Yea, yea, tis wel; I must be cald rubbish, kitchin-stuffe, for a sort of knaues.

Firke. Nay, dame, you shall not weepe and waile in woe for me. Master, Ile stay no longer; here's a vennentorie of my shop-tooles. Adue, master; Hodge, farewel.

55 *Hodge.* Nay, stay, Firke; thou shalt not go alone.

Wife. I pray, let them goe; there be mo maides then Mawkin, more men then Hodge, and more fooles then Firke.

Firke. Fooles? Nailes! if I tarry nowe, I would my guts might be turnd to shoo-thread.

---

33. *journeyman* E. — 35. *butten-hole* C. — 38. *at* om. E. — 44. *Am not I* DE. — 45. *those* DE. — 53. *a eventory* C, *an enuentory* DE. — 54. *maister* C. — 58. *Fuoles* C; *gute* E.

Hodge. And if I stay, I pray God I may be turnd to a 60
Turke, and set in Finsbury for boyes to shoot at. — Come,
Firk.

Eyre. Stay, my fine knaues, you armes of my trade, you
pillars of my profession. What, shal a tittle-tattles words
make you forsake Simon Eyre? — Auaunt, kitchin-stuffe! 65
Rip, you brown-bread Tannikin; out of my sight! Moue me
not! Haue not I tane you from selling tripes in Eastcheape,
and set you in my shop, and made you haile-fellowe with
Simon Eyre, the shoomaker? And now do you deale thus with
my Journeymen? Looke, you powder-beefe-queane, on the 70
face of Hodge, heers a face for a Lord.

Firk. And heers a face for any Lady in christendome.

Eyre. Rip, you chitterling, auaunt! Boy, bid the tapster
of the Bores-head fil me a doozen cannes of beere for my
iourneymen.   75

Firk. A doozen cans? O, braue! Hodge, now Ile stay.

Eyre. (*In a low voice to the boy*) And the knaue fils any
more then two, he payes for them. (*Exit Boy. Loud.*) A
doozen cans of beere for my iourneymen. (*Re-enter Boy.*) Here,
you mad Mesopotamians, wash your liuers with this liquour. 80
Where be the odde ten? No more, Madge, no more. —
Wel saide. Drinke and to work! — What worke dost thou,
Hodge? what work?

Hodge. I am a making a paire of shooes for my Lord
Maiors daughter, mistresse Rose.   85

Firk. And I a paire of shooes for Sybill, my Lords maid.
I deale with her.

Eyre. Sybil? Fie, defile not thy fine workmanly fingers
with the feete of kitchinstuffe and basting-ladles. Ladies of
the Court, fine Ladies, my lads, commit their feete to our 90
apparelling; put grosse worke to Hans. Yarke and seame,
yarke and seame!

Firk. For yarking and seaming let me alone, and I
come toot.

64. *my*] *me* C; *word* CDE. — 66. *tanniking* C. — 68. *make* DE. —
73. *Rip you, chitterling* A. — 77 seqq. Stage-directions added by Fr. —
79. *Heare you, mad* AB. — 84. *am making* DE. — 89. *feet of kitchingstuff* DE.

95   *Hodge.* Wel, maister, al this is from the bias. Do you
remember the ship my fellow Hans told you of? The skipper
and he are both drinking at the Swan. Here be the Portigues
to giue earnest. If you go through with it, you cannot choose
but be a Lord at least.

100   *Firk.* Nay, dame, if my master proue not a Lord, and you
a Ladie, hang me.

Wife. Yea, like inough, if you may loiter and tipple thus.

Firke. Tipple, dame? No, we haue beene bargaining with
Skellum Skanderbag: can you Dutch spreaken for a ship of
105   silk Cipresse, laden with sugar Candie.

Enter the Boy with a velvet coate and an Aldermans gowne.
                    AYRE *puts it on.*

Eyre. Peace, Firk; silence, Tittle - tattle! Hodge, Ile go
through with it. Heers a seale - ring, and I haue sent for a
garded gown and a damask casock. See where it comes;
looke heere, Maggy; help me, Firk; apparrel me, Hodge;
110   silke and satten, you mad Philistines, silke and satten.

Firk. Ha, ha, my maister wil be as proud as a dogge in
a dublet, al in beaten damaske and veluet.

Eyre. Softly, Firke, for rearing of the nap, and wearing
threadbare my garments. How doest thou like mee, Firke?
115   How do I looke, my fine Hodge?

Hodge. Why, now you looke like your self, master. I
warrant you, ther's few in the city, but wil giue you the wal,
and come vpon you with the right worshipful.

Firke. Nailes, my master lookes like a threadbare cloake
120   new turn'd and drest. Lord, Lord, to see what good raiment
doth! Dame, dame, are you not enamoured?

Eyre. How saist thou, Maggy, am I not brisk? Am I
not fine?

Wife. Fine? By my troth, sweet hart, very fine! By my
125   troth, I neuer likte thee so wel in my life, sweete heart; but
let that passe. I warrant, there be many women in the citie

---

haue not such handsome husbands, but only for their apparell; but let that passe too.

Enter HANS *and Skipper.*

Hans. Godden day, mester. Dis be de skipper dat heb de skip van marchandice; de commodity ben good; nempt it, 130 master, nempt it.

Eyre. Godamercy, Hans; welcome, skipper. Where lies this ship of marchandice?

Skipper. De skip ben in reuere; dor be van Sugar, cyuet, almonds, cambricke, and a towsand towsand tings, gotz sacra- 135 ment; nempt it, mester: ye sal heb good copen.

Firk. To him, maister! O sweete maister! O sweet wares! Prunes, almonds, suger-candy, carrat-roots, turnups, o braue fatting meate! Let not a man buye a nutmeg but your selfe.

Eyre. Peace, Firke! Come, Skipper, Ile go aboord with 140 you. — Hans, haue you made him drinke?

Skipper. Yaw, yaw, ic heb veale gedrunck.

Eyre. Come, Hans, follow me. Skipper, thou shalt haue my countenance in the Cittie.   [*Exeunt.*

Firk. Yaw, heb veale gedrunck, quoth a. They may well 145 be called butter-boxes, when they drinke fat veale and thick beare too. But come, dame, I hope you'le chide vs no more.

Wife. No, faith, Firke; no, perdy, Hodge. I do feele honour creepe upon me, and which is more, a certaine rising in my flesh; but let that passe.   150

Firk. Rising in your flesh do you feele say you? I, you may be with childe, but why should not my maister feele a rising in his flesh, hauing a gowne and a gold ring on? But you are such a shrew, you'le soone pull him downe.

Wife. Ha, ha! prethee, peace! Thou mak'st my worshippe 155 laugh; but let that passe. Come, Ile go in; Hodge, prethee, goe before me; Firke, follow me.

Firke. Firke doth follow; Hodge, passe out in state. [*Exeunt.*

---

130. *marchandize* DE. — 131. *mester* CDE. — 133. *merchandize* DE. — 134. *rouere* Qq., *civit* DE. — 135. *gots* CDE. — 136. *yo* A; *hab* DE. — 138. *Almons* C; *carret-roots, turnips* DE. — 140. *abroade* AB. — 142. *gedrunke* CDE. — 145. *gedrunke* CD, *gedrunk* E. — 151. *you say* DE.

SCENE II.

Enter LINCOLNE *and* DODGER.

Lincolne. How now, good Dodger, whats the newes in
    Dodger. My Lord, vpon the eighteenth day of May [France?
The French and English were preparde to fight;
Each side with eager furie gaue the signe
5 Of a most hot encounter. Fiue long howres
Both armies fought together; at the length
The lot of victorie fel on our sides.
Twelue thousand of the Frenchmen that day dide,
Foure thousand English, and no man of name
10 But Captaine Hyam and yong Ardington,
Two gallant gentlemen, I knew them well.
    Lincolne. But Dodger, prethee, tell me, in this fight
How did my cozen Lacie beare himselfe?
    Dodger. My Lord, your cosen Lacie was not there.
15   *Lincolne.* Not there?
    Dodger.   No, my good Lord.
    Lincolne.   Sure, thou mistakest.
I saw him shipt, and a thousand eies beside
Were witnesses of the farewels which he gaue,
When I, with weeping eies, bid him adew.
Dodger, take heede.
    Dodger.   My Lord, I am aduis'de,
20 That what I spake is true: to proue it so,
His cosen Askew, that supplide his place,
Sent me for him from France, that secretly
He might conuey himselfe thither.
    Lincolne.   Ist euen so?
Dares he so carelessly venture his life,
25 Upon the indignation of a king?
Has he despis'd my loue, and spurn'd those fauours
Which I with prodigall hand powr'd on his head?
He shall repent his rashnes with his soule;
Since of my loue he makes no estimate,

SCENE II. [*Scene 8. London. A room in Lincoln's house.*] Fr. —
2. *eighteene* AB. — 17. *witness* CDE, cp. Henr. VIII., II. 1. 17, and see
S. Walker, *Versif.*, p. 243 seqq. and Abbott, s. 471. — 20. *speake* C, *speak*
DE. — 23. *hither* Qq.

He make him wish he had not knowne my hate.   30
Thou hast no other newes?
    Dodger.   None else, my Lord.
    Lincolne.   None worse I know thou hast. — Procure the king
To crowne his giddie browes with ample honors,
Send him cheefe Colonell, and all my hope
Thus to be dasht! But tis in vaine to grieue,   35
One euill cannot a worse releeue.
Upon my life, I haue found out his plot;
That old dog, Loue, that fawnd upon him so,
Loue to that puling girle, his faire - cheek't Rose,
The Lord Maiors daughter, hath distracted him,   40
And in the fire of that loues lunacie
Hath he burnt vp himselfe, consum'd his credite,
Lost the kings loue, yea, and I feare, his life,
Onely to get a wanton to his wife.
Dodger, it is so.   45
    Dodger.   I feare so, my good Lord.
    Lincolne.   It is so — nay, sure it cannot be!
I am at my wits end. Dodger!
    Dodger.   Yea, my Lord.
    Lincolne.   Thou art acquainted with my nephewes haunts;
Spend this gold for thy paines; goe seeke him out;
Watch at my Lord Maiors — there if he liue,   50
Dodger, thou shalt be sure to meete with him.
Prethee, be diligent. — Lacie, thy name
Liu'd once in honour, now tis dead in shame. —
Be circumspect.   [*Exit.*
    Dodger.   I warrant you, my Lord.   [*Exit.*

SCENE III.

Enter LORD MAIOR *and Master* SCOTTE.

L. Maior.   Good maister Scot, I haue beene bolde with you,
To be a witnesse to a wedding - knot

---

36. Is *worse* used as a disyllable here? *worse one* Fr., *more worse* pres.
Edd. conj.; cp. Lear, II. 2. 155: *My sister may receive it much more worse.*
— 47. *end, Dodger* Qq. — 48. *acquinted* E. — 53. *tis* wanting in Qq.
    SCENE III. [*Scene 9. London. A room in the Lord Mayor's house.*] Fr.
Stage - dir. *Scot* CDE. — 2. *weding* C.

Betwixt yong maister Hammon and my daughter.
O, stand aside; see where the Louers come.

Enter HAMMON *and* ROSE.

5   *Rose.* Can it be possible, you loue me so?
No, no, within those eie‑bals I espie
Apparant likelihoods of flattery.
Pray now, let go my hand.
    Hammon.   Sweete mistris Rose,
Misconstrue not my words, nor misconceiue
10 Of my affection, whose deuoted soule
Sweares that I loue thee dearer then my heart.
    Rose. As deare as your owne heart? I iudge it right,
Men loue their hearts best when th'are out of sight.
    Hammon. I loue you, by this hand.
    Rose.   Yet hands off now!
15 If flesh be fraile, how weake and frail's your vowe!
    Hammon. Then by my life I sweare.
    Rose.   Then do not brawle;
One quarrell looseth wife and life and all.
Is not your meaning thus?
    Hammon.   In faith, you iest.
    Rose. Loue loues to sport; therefore leaue loue, y'are best.
20 *L. Maior.* What? square they, maister Scot?
    Scot.   Sir, neuer doubt,
Louers are quickly in, and quickly out.
    Hammon. Sweet Rose, be not so strange in fansying me.
Nay, neuer turne aside, shunne not my sight:
I am not growne so fond, to fond my loue
25 On any that shall quit it with disdaine;
If you wil loue me, so — if not, farewell.
    L. Maior. Why, how now, louers, are you both agreede?
    Hammon. Yes, faith, my Lord.
    L. Maior.   Tis well, giue me your hand.
Giue me yours, daughter. — How now, both pull back!
30 What meanes this, girle?

8. *Pray, now let* Qq. — 15. *frial* E. — 28—30. *Tis well . . . girle* two
lines in Qq., the first ending at *daughter*. — 29. *now*] *not* C.

Rose.   I meane to liue a maide.

Hammon. But not to die one; pawse, ere that be said. [*Aside.*

L. Maior. Wil you stil crosse me, still be obstinate?

Hammon. Nay, chide her not, my Lord, for doing well;
If she can liue an happie virgins life,
'Tis farre more blessed then to be a wife.   35

Rose. Say, sir, I cannot: I haue made a vow,
Who euer be my husband, tis not you.

L. Maior. Your tongue is quicke; but M. Hamond, know,
I bade you welcome to another end.

Hammon. What, would you haue me pule and pine and pray,   40
With 'louely ladie', 'mistris of my heart',
'Pardon your seruant', and the rimer play,
Rayling on Cupid and his tyrants-dart;
Or shal I undertake some martiall spoile,
Wearing your gloue at turney and at tilt,   45
And tel how many gallants I unhorst —
Sweete, wil this pleasure you?

Rose.   Yea, when wilt begin?
What, louerimes, man? Fie on that deadly sinne!

L. Maior. If you wil haue her, Ile make her agree.

Hammon. Enforced loue is worse than hate to me.   50
(*Aside.*) There is a wench keepes shop in the Old-Change,
To her wil I; it is not wealth I seeke,
I haue enough, and wil preferre her loue
Before the world. — (*Loud.*) My good Lord Maior, adew.
Old loue for me, I haue no lucke with new.   [*Exit.* 55

L. Maior. Now, mammet, you haue wel behau'd your selfe,
But you shal curse your coynes, if I liue. —
Whose within there? See you conuay your mistris
Straight to th'Old-Forde! Ile keepe you straight enough.
Fore God, I would haue sworne the puling girle   60
Would willingly accepted Hammons loue;

47. *pleasure*] *please* Fr., but read *'gin* for *begin*, cp. Abbott, s. 460;
Yea] *Yes* BDE. — 51. 54. Stage-dir. added by Fr. — 58. *Who's* DE. —
61. *accept* DE; Fr. (p. 63) proposes *accept of*, but cp. Shak. Coriolanus IV.
6. 35: *We would by this, to all our lamentation, If he had gone forth con-*
sul, found it so, and Edw. III., IV. 5. 101 seqq.: *The royal king .. Would not*
alone safe-conduct give to them, But with all bounty feasted them and theirs.

3

But banish him, my thoughts! — Go, minion, in! [*Exit Rose.*
Now tel me, master Scot, would you haue thought
That master Simon Eyre, the shoomaker,

65   Had beene of wealth to buy such marchandize?
      Scot. Twas wel, my Lord, your honour and my selfe
Grew partners with him; for your bils of lading
Shew that Eyres gains in one commoditie
Rise at the least to ful three thousand pound

70   Besides like gaine in other marchandize.
      L. Maior. Wel, he shal spend some of his thousands now,
For I haue sent for him to the Guild Hall.

Enter EYRE.

See, where he comes. — Good morrow, master Eyre.
      Eyre. Poore Simon Eyre, my Lord, your shoomaker.

75   *L. Maior.* Wel, wel, it likes your selfe to terme you so.

Enter DODGER.

Now, M. Dodger, whats the news with you?
      Dodger. Ide gladly speake in priuate to your honour.
      L. Maior. You shal, you shal. — Master Eyre and M. Scot,
I haue some businesse with this gentleman;

80   I pray, let me intreate you to walke before
To the Guild Hal; Ile follow presently.
Master Eyre, I hope ere noone to call you Shiriffe.
      Eyre. I would not care, my Lord, if you might cal me
king of Spaine. — Come, master Scot. [*Exeunt* EYRE *and* SCOT.

85   *L. Maior.* Now, Maister Dodger, whats the newes you bring?
      Dodger. The Earle of Lincolne by me greets your Lordship,
And earnestly requests you, if you can,
Informe him, where his nephew Lacie keepes.
      L. Maior. Is not his nephew Lacie now in France?

90   *Dodger.* No, I assure your Lordship, but disguisde
Lurkes here in London.

---

63. *maister* C. — 64. *maister* C; *Eyer* E. — 65. *merchandize* CDE.
— 70. *merchandize* DE. — 73, 78 *maister* C. — 75. *Enter Dodger.*
Put after l. 76 in AB. — 77. *honor* C. — 82, 84, 95. *maister* C. —
82. *Sheriffe* C, *Sherife* DE. — 84. Stage - dir. added by Fr.

L. Maior.   London? ist euen so?
It may be; but vpon my faith and soule,
I know not where he liues, or whether he liues:
So tel my Lord of Lincolne. — Lurch in London?
Well, master Dodger, you perhaps may start him;   95
Be but the meanes to rid him into France,
He giue you a dozen angels for your paines:
So much I loue his honour, hate his Nephew,
And, prethee, so informe thy lord from me.
     Dodger. I take my leaue.   [*Exit* DODGER. 100
     L. Maior.   Farewell, good master Dodger.
Lacie in London? I dare pawne my life,
My daughter knowes thereof, and for that cause
Denide yong M. Hammon in his loue.
Wel, I am glad, I sent her to Old-Forde.
Gods Lord, tis late; to Guild Hall I must hie;   105
I know my brethren stay my companie.   [*Exit.*

SCENE IV.

Enter FIRKE, EYRES *Wife,* HANS, *and* ROGER.

Wife. Thou goest too fast for me, Roger. O, Firke!
Firke. I, forsooth.
Wife. I pray thee, runne — doe you heare? — runne to
Guild Hall, and learne if my husband, master Eyre, wil take
that worshipfull vocation of M. Shiriffe vpon him. Hie thee,   5
good Firke.
Firke. Take it? Well, I goe; and he should not take it,
Firke sweares to forsweare him. Yes, forsooth, I goe to Guild Hall.
Wife. Nay, when? thou art too compendious and tedious.
Firke. O rare, your excellence is full of eloquence; how   10
like a new cart-wheele my dame speakes, and she lookes like
an old musty ale-bottle going to scalding.

94. *Lurk* CDE. — 100. *M. Dodger* CDE. — 101. *Lacie]* *Lacies* C,
Lacy's DE. — 103. *Denied* D; *Maister* C, *Master* DE. — 106. *stay] lack* CDE.
     SCENE IV. [*Scene* 10. *London. A room in Eyre's house.*] Fr. —
Stage-dir. *and* om. DE. — 1. *O, Firke* wanting in AB. — 4. *M. Eyre* CDE.
— 5. *Sheriffe* C, *Sherife* D, *Sheriff* E. — 9. *th'art* CDE; *too] two* D, *to* E;
tedious C.

Wife. Nay, when? thou wilt make me melancholy.

Firke. God forbid, your worship should fall into that
15 humour; — I runne.   [*Exit.*

Wife. Let me see now, Roger and Hans.

Hodge. I, forsooth, dame -- mistris I should say, but
the old terme so stickes to the roofe of my mouth, I can
hardly lick it off.

20 *Wife.* Euen what thou wilt, good Roger; dame is a faire
name for any honest christian; but let that passe. How dost
thou, Hans?

Hans. Mee tanck you, vro.

Wife. Wel, Hans and Roger, you see, God hath blest your
25 master, and, perdie, if euer he comes to be M. Shiriffe of
London — as we are al mortal — you shal see, I wil haue
some odde thing or other in a corner for you: I wil not
be your backe - friend; but let that passe. Hans, pray thee,

· *Hans.* Yaw, ic sal, vro.   [tie my shooe.
30 *Wife.* Roger, thou knowst the length of my foote; as it
is none of the biggest, so I thanke God, it is handsome
enough; prethee, let me haue a paire of shooes made, corke,
good Roger, woodden heele, too.

Hodge. You shall.

35 *Wife.* Art thou acquainted with neuer a fardingale - maker,
nor a French - hoode - maker? I must enlarge my bumme,
ha, ha! How shall I looke in a hoode, I wonder! Perdy,
odly, I thinke.

Roger. As a catte out of a pillorie: verie wel, I warrant
40 you, mistresse.

Wife. Indeede, all flesh is grasse; and, Roger, canst thou
tel where I may buye a good haire?

Roger. Yes, forsooth, at the poulterers in Gracious - street.

Wife. Thou art an vngratious wag; perdy, I meane a
45 false haire for my periwig.

---

17. *Hodge*] *H.* (i. e. *Hodge*) A, *R.* (i. e. *Roger*) B, *Ro.* CDE. — 21. *any*]
my DE. — 23. *Me* CDE. — 25. *come* CDE; *maister Sheriffe* C, *M. Sherife*
DE. — 29. *ic*] *il* DE. — 35. *Art*] *Atr* E; *thou not acq.* DE. — 36. *bum* E.
— 37. *ha, ha, ha* CDE. — 45. *perewig* CDE.

Roger. Why, mistris, the next time I cut my beard, you
shall haue the shauings of it; but they are all true haires.

Wife. It is verie hot, I must get me a fan or else a maske.

Roger. So you had neede, to hide your wicked face.

Wife. Fie vpon it, how costly this world's calling is; perdy,   50
but that it is one of the wonderfull works of God, I would
not deale with it. Is not Firke come yet? Hans, bee not so
sad, let it passe and vanish, as my husbands worshippe saies.

Hans. Ick bin vrolicke, lot see yow soo.

Roger. Mistris, wil you drinke a pipe of tobacco?   55

Wife. Oh, fie uppon it, Roger, perdy! These filthie tobacco
-pipes are the most idle slauering bables that euer I felt. Out
uppon it! God blesse vs, men looke not like men that vse them.

Enter RAFE, *being lame.*

Roger. What, fellow Rafe? Mistres, looke here, lanes
husband! Why, how now, lame? Hans, make much of him,   60
hees a brother of our trade, a good workeman, and a tall

Hans. You be welcome, broder.   [souldier.

Wife. Pardie, I knew him not. How dost thou, good Rafe?
I am glad to see thee wel.

Rafe. I would to God, you saw me, dame, as wel   65
As when I went from London into France.

Wife. Trust mee, I am sorie, Rafe, to see thee impotent.
Lord, how the warres haue made him sunburnt! The left leg
is not wel; twas a faire gift of God, the infirmitie tooke not
hold a litle higher, considering thou camest from France; but   70
let that passe.

Rafe. I am glad to see you wel, and I reioyce
To heare that God hath blest my master so
Since my departure.

Wife. Yea, truly, Rafe, I thanke my maker; but let that passe.   75

Roger. And, sirra Rafe, what newes, what newes in France?

Rafe. Tel me, good Roger, first, what newes in England?
How does my lane? When didst thou see my wife?

46. *time that I* CDE. — 47. *they*] *mine* CDE. — 54. *you* C. — 60. *now*
om. A. — 65. *to* wanting in Qq. — 68. *The*] *Thy* DE. — 69. *a*] *the* DE;
guift C. — 73. *maister* C.

Where liues my poore heart? Sheel be poore indeed,
80 Now I want limbs to get whereon to feed.

   Roger. Limbs? Hast thou not hands, man? Thou shalt
neuer see a shoomaker want bread, though he haue but three
fingers on a hand.

   Rafe. Yet all this while I heare not of my Iane.

85   *Wife.* O Rafe, your wife, — perdie, we knowe not whats
become of her. She was here a while, and because she
was married, grewe more stately then became her; I checkt
her, and so forth; away she flung, neuer returned, nor saide
bih nor bah; and, Rafe, you knowe, 'ka me, ka thee'. And
90 so, as I tell ye — Roger, is not Firke come yet?

   Roger. No, forsooth.

   Wife. And so, indeede, we heard not of her, but I heare
she liues in London; but let that passe. If she had wanted,
shee might haue opened her case to me or my husband, or
95 to any of my men; I am sure, theres not any of them, perdie,
but would haue done her good to his power. Hans, looke,
if Firke be come.

   Hans. Yaw, ik sal, vro.   *[Exit* HANS.

   Wife. And so, as I saide — but, Rafe, why dost thou
100 weepe? Thou knowest that naked wee came out of our
mothers wombe, and naked we must returne; and, therefore,
thanke God for al things.

   Roger. No, faith, Iane is a straunger heere; but, Rafe,
pull vp a good heart, I knowe thou hast one. Thy wife,
105 man, is in London; one tolde mee, hee sawe her a while
agoe verie braue and neate; weele ferret her out, and London
holde her.

   Wife. Alas, poore soule, hees ouercome with sorrowe; he
does but as I doe, weepe for the losse of any good thing.
110 But, Rafe, get thee in, call for some meate and drinke, thou
shalt find me worshipful towards thee.

   Rafe. I thanke you, dame; since I want lims and lands,
Ile trust to God, my good friends, and my hands.   *[Exit.*

   95. *there is* CDE. — 98. *ik*] *it* A. — 106. *an London* DE. — 112. *limbs*
DE. — 113. *Ile to God, my good friends, and to these my hands* AB,
I'll trust to God, my good friends, and to my hands CDE; *and my
hands* Fr.

Enter HANS *and* FIRKE, *running.*

Firke. Runne, good Hans! O Hodge, O mistres! Hodge, heaue vp thine eares; mistresse, smugge vp your lookes; on 115 with your best apparell; my maister is chosen, my master is called, nay, condemn'd by the crie of the countrie to be Shiriffe of the Citie for this famous yeare nowe to come. And time now being, a great many men in blacke gownes were askt for their voyces and their hands, and my master had 120 al their fists about his eares presently, and they cried 'I, I, I, I,' — and so I came away —

　　　　Wherefore without all other grieue,
　　　　I doe salute you mistresse shrieue.

Hans. Yaw, my mester is de groot man, de shrieue.　　　125

Roger. Did not I tell you, mistris? Nowe I may boldly say: Good morrow to your worship.

Wife. Good morrow, good Roger. I thanke you, my good people all. — Firke, hold vp thy hand: heer's a three-peny -peece for thy tidings.　　　130

Firke. Tis but three-halfe-pence, I thinke. Yes, tis three -pence, I smel the Rose.

Roger. But, mistresse, be rulde by me, and doe not speake so pulingly.

Firke. Tis her worship speakes so, and not she. No, faith, 135 mistresse, speake mee in the olde key: 'too it, Firke', 'there, good Firke', 'plie your businesse, Hodge', 'Hodge, with a full mouth', 'Ile fill your bellies with good cheere, til they crie twang.'

Enter Simon Eyre, wearing a gold chaine.

Hans. See, myn lieuer broder, heer compt my meester.

Wife. Welcome home, maister shrieue; I pray God con- 140 tinue you in health and wealth.

Eyre. See here, my Maggy, a chaine, a gold chaine for Simon Eyre. I shal make thee a Lady; heer's a French hood for thee; on with it, on with it! dresse thy browes with this flap of a shoulder of mutton, to make thee looke louely. Where 145 be my fine men? Roger, Ile make ouer my shop and tooles

---

116. *maister* C. — 118. *Sheriffe* C, *Sherife* DE. — 120. *maister* C. — 123, 124. First printed as verse by Fr. — 125. *meester* CDE; *goot* CDE. — 129. *threepence* C. — 139. *myn*] *mine* CDE; *heere* C, *here* DE.

to thee; Firke, thou shalt be the foreman; Hans, thou shalt
haue an hundred for twentie.   Bee as mad knaues as your
maister Sim Eyre hath bin, and you shall liue to be Sheriues
150 of London. — How dost thou like me, Margerie?   Prince am
I none, yet am I princely borne.   Firke, Hodge, and Hans!
 All 3.   I forsooth, what saies your worship, master Sherife?
 Eyre.   Worship and honour, you Babilonian knaues, for
the Gentle Craft.   But I forgot my selfe, I am bidden by my
155 Lord Maior to dinner to Old-Ford; hees gone before, I must
after.   Come, Madge, on with your trinkets!   Nowe, my true
Troians, my fine Firke, my dapper Hodge, my honest Hans,
some deuice, some odde crochets, some morris, or such like,
for the honour of the gentlemen shooemakers.   Meete me at
160 Old-Ford, you know my minde.   Come, Madge, away.   Shutte
vp the shop, knaues, and make holiday.   [*Exeunt.*
 Firke.   O rare! o braue!   Come, Hodge; follow me, Hans;
 Weele be with them for a morris-daunce.   [*Exeunt.*

SCENE V.

Enter LORD MAIOR, EYRE, *his* WIFE *in a French hood,* SIBILL,
and other seruants.

 L. Maior.   Trust mee, you are as welcome to Old-Ford
As I my selfe.
 Wife.   Truely, I thanke your Lordship.
 L. Maior.   Would our bad cheere were worth the thanks
               [you giue.
5 *Eyre.*   Good cheere, my Lord Maior, fine cheere!   A fine
house, fine walles, all fine and neat.
 L. Maior.   Now, by my troth, Ile tel thee, maister Eyre,
It does me good and al my brethren,
That such a madcap fellow as thy selfe
10 Is entred into our societie.

  149. *master Simon Eyr* E; *Sheriffes* C, *Sherifes* DE. — 152. *master*]
mistris ABCD; *Sherif* E. — 153. *honor* C; *ye* CDE. — 154. *by*] *to* DE.
— 157. *dapar* E. — 159. *honor* C; *gentlemen*] *gentle* AB, *gentleman* C;
Shoomakers C, *Shoemakers* DE.
  SCENE V. [*Scene* 11.   *Oldford.   A room.*] Fr. — Stage-dir. *Wife,
Sibill in a French hood* AB. — 2. *I* om. CDE. — 8. *brethren* used as a
trisyllable; *brethren too,* Fr,

Wife. I, but, my Lord, hee must learne nowe to putte on grauitie.

Eyre. Peace, Maggy, a fig for grauitie! When I go to Guild Hal in my scarlet gowne, Ile look as demurely as a saint, and speake as grauely as a Iustice of peace; but now I   15
am here at Old-Foord, at my good Lord Maiors house, let it go by, vanish, Maggy, Ile be merrie; away with flip-flap, these fooleries, these gulleries. What, hunnie? Prince am I inone, yet am I princely borne. What sayes my Lord Maior?   20

L. Maior. Ha, ha, ha! I had rather then a thousand pound, I had an heart but halfe so light as yours.

Eyre. Why, what should I do, my Lord? A pound of care paies not a dram of debt. Hum, lets be merry, whiles we are yong; old age, sacke and sugar will steale vpon vs, ere   25
we be aware.

L. Maior. Its wel done; mistris Eyre, pray, giue good counsell To my daughter.

Wife. I hope, mistris Rose wil haue the grace to take nothing thats bad.   30

L. Maior. Pray God, she do; for ifaith, mistris Eyre, I would bestow vpon that peeuish girle A thousand marks more then I meane to giue her, Upon condition sheed be rulde by me; The Ape still crosseth me. There came of late   35
A proper gentleman of fair reuenewes, Whom gladly I would call sonne in law: But my fine cockney would haue none of him. You'le proue a cockscombe for it, ere you die: A courtier, or no man must please your eie.   40

Eyre. Be rulde, sweete Rose: th'art ripe for a man. Marrie not with a boy that has no more haire on his face then thou hast on thy cheekes. A courtier, wash, go by, stand not vppon pisherie - pasherie: those silken fellowes are but painted images,

---

18. *those f.* E. — 19. *am princely* CDE. — 21, 22. Printed as prose in CDE; *ha, ha, ha* stands for two syllables, and *I had* is to be contracted (*I'd*). — 22. *but halfe* om. in E. — 23. *while* CDE. — 27, 28. Printed as pross in Qq. — 34. *she be* CDE. — 37. *glady* C; read: *glad[e]ly; my son* Fr. conj. — 38. *cocknew* E. — 44. *pointed* B.

45   outsides, outsides, Rose; their inner linings are torne. No,
my fine mouse, marry me with a Gentleman Grocer like my
Lord Maior, your father; a grocer is a sweete trade: plums,
plums. Had I a sonne or daughter should marrie out of the
generation and bloud of the shoemakers, he should packe;
50   what, the Gentle Trade is a liuing for a man through Europe,
through the world.

   A noyse within of a Taber and a Pipe.
 L. Maior. What noyse is this?
 Eyre. O my Lord Maior, a crue of good fellowes that for
loue to your honour are come hither with a morris - dance.
55   Come in, my Mesopotamians, cheerely!

 Enter HODGE, HANS, RAPH, FIRKE, *and other Shooemakers, in a*
  morris; after a little dauncing the LORD MAIOR *speakes:*
 L. Maior. Maister Eyre, are al these shoemakers?
 Eyre. Al cordwainers, my good Lord Maior.
 Rose. (*Aside.*) How like my Lacie lookes yond shooemaker!
 Haunce. (*Aside.*) O that I durst but speake unto my loue!
60   *L. Maior.* Sibil, go fetch some wine to make these drinke.
You are al welcome.
 All. We thanke your Lordship.

  ROSE *takes a cup of wine and goes to* HAUNCE.
 Rose. For his sake whose faire shape thou representst,
Good friend, I drinke to thee.
65   *Hans.* Ic bedancke, good frister.
 Eyres Wife. I see, mistris Rose, you do not want iudgement;
you haue drunke to the properest man I keepe.
 Firke. Here bee some haue done their parts to be as
proper as he.
70   *L. Maior.* Wel, urgent busines cals me backe to London:
Good fellowes, first go in and taste our cheare;
And to make merrie as you homeward go,
Spend these two angels in beere at Stratford-Boe.
 Eyre. To these two, my madde lads, Sim Eyre ads an-

  51. *thorow* DE. — Stage-dir. *and Pipe.* E. — 53. *followes* C. —
54. *honor* C. — 58, 59. (*Aside.*) added by Fr. — 61. Stage-dir. *the cup* E.
— 65. *trister* DE. — 73. *angels* used as a monosyllable; *Bo.* E. — 74. *Simon*
CDE; *adds* CDE.

other; then cheerely, Firke; tickle it, Haunce, and al for the 75
honour of shoemakers. [*All goe dauncing out.*

L. Maior. Come, maister Eyre, lets haue your companie.
Rose. Sibil, what shal I do? [*Exeunt.*
Sibil. Why, whats the matter?
Rose. That Haunce the shoemaker is my loue Lacie, 80
Disguisde in that attire to find me out.
How should I find the meanes to speake with him?
Sibil. What, mistris, neuer feare; I dare venter my maiden-
head to nothing, and thats great oddes, that Haunce the
Dutchman, when we come to London, shal not onely see and 85
speake with you, but in spight of al your fathers pollicies
steale you away and marrie you. Will not this please you?
Rose. Do this, and euer be assured of my loue.
Sibil. Away, then, and follow your father to London, lest
your absence cause him to suspect something: 90
>   To-morrow, if my counsel be obayde,
>   Ile binde you prentise to the gentle trade. [*Exeunt.*

ACT IV.

SCENE I.

Enter IANE *in a Semsters shop, working; and* HAMMON, *muffled,
at another doore; he stands aloofe.*

Hammon. Yonders the shop, and there my faire loue sits.
Shees faire and louely, but she is not mine.
O, would she were! Thrise haue I courted her,
Thrise hath my hand beene moistned with her hand,
Whilst my poore famisht eies do feed on that 5
Which made them famish. I am infortunate:
I stil loue one, yet nobody loues me.
I muse, in other men what women see,
That I so want! Fine mistris Rose was coy,
And this too curious! Oh, no, she is chaste, 10

77. *let haue you companie* C. — 79. *what'e matter* E. — 83. *venture*
E. — 86. *polices* DE. — 89. *least* C. — 91. *obaide* C. — 92. [*Exeunt.*]
added by Fr.
ACT IV. SCENE I. [*Scene* 12. *London. A street*] Fr.

And for she thinkes me wanton, she denies
To cheare my cold heart with her sunnie eies.
How prettily she workes, oh prettie hand!
Oh happie worke! It doth me good to stand
15 Unseene to see her. Thus I oft haue stood
In frostie euenings, a light burning by her,
Enduring biting cold, only to eie her.
One onely look hath seem'd as rich to me
As a kings crowne; such is loues lunacie.
20 Muffeled Ile passe along, and by that trie
Whether she know me.

Iane.   Sir, what ist you buy?
What ist you lacke, sir, callico, or lawne,
Fine cambricke shirts, or bands, what will you buy?

Hammon. (*Aside.*) That which thou wilt not sell. Faith, yet
25 How do you sell this handkercher?   [Ile trie:
Iane.   Good cheape.
Hammon. And how these ruffes?
Iane.   Cheape too.
Hammon.   And how this band?
Iane. Cheape too.
Hammon.   All cheape; how sell you then this hand?
Iane. My handes are not to be solde.
Hammon.   To be giuen then!
Nay, faith, I come to buy.
Iane.   But none knowes when.
30 *Hammon.* Good sweete, leaue worke a little while; lets play.
Iane. I cannot liue by keeping holliday.
Hammon. Ile pay you for the time which shall be lost.
Iane. With me you shall not be at so much cost.
Hammon. Look, how you wound this cloth, so you wound me.
35 *Iane.* It may be so.
Hammon.   Tis so.
Iane.   What remedie?
Hammon. Nay, faith, you are too coy.
Iane.   Let goe my hand.

12. *cold*] *could* E. — 19. *lover's* C. — 24 (*Aside.*) added by Fr. — 28,
28. *To be ... buy.* One line in Qq., divided by Fr.; *to be* used as a monosyllable (twice).

Hammon.   I will do any task at your command,
I would let goe this beautie, were I not
In mind to disobey you by a power
That controlles kings: I loue you!   40
　Iane.   So, now part.
　Hammon.   With hands I may, but neuer with my heart.
In faith, I loue you.
　Iane.   I beleeue, you doe.
　Hammon.   Shall a true loue in me breede hate in you?
　Iane.   I hate you not.
　Hammon.   Then you must loue?
　Iane.   I doe.
What are you better now? I loue not you.   45
　Hammon.   All this, I hope, is but a womans fray
That means: come to me, when she cries: away!
In earnest, mistris, I do not iest,
A true chaste loue hath entred in my brest.
I loue you dearely, as I loue my life,   50
I loue you as a husband loues a wife;
That, and no other loue, my loue requires.
Thy wealth, I know, is little; my desires
Thirst not for gold. Sweete, beautous Iane, whats mine
Shall, if thou make my selfe thine, all be thine.   55
Say, iudge, what is thy sentence, life or death?
Mercie or crueltie lies in thy breath.
　Iane.   Good Sir, I do beleeue you loue me well;
For tis a seely conquest, seely pride
For one like you — I meane a gentleman —   60
To boast that by his loue-tricks he hath brought
Such and such women to his amorous lure;
I thinke you do not so, yet many doe,
And make it euen a very trade to wooe.
I could be coy, as many women be,   65
Feede you with sunne-shine smiles and wanton lookes,

---

41. *hand* E. — 44. *I doe . . . you.* One line in Qq., divided by Fr.
— 48. *mistris* to be pronounced as a trisyllable; *for I* Fr. — 50. *loues*
E; *as I do my* CDE.

But I detest witchcraft; say that I
Doe constantly beleeue, you constant haue —
 Hammon. Why dost thou not beleeue me?
 Iane.   I beleeue you;
70 But yet, good Sir, because I will not grieue you
With hopes to taste fruite which will neuer fall,
In simple truth this is the summe of all:
My husband liues, at least, I hope he liues.
Prest was he to these bitter warres in France;
75 Bitter they are to me by wanting him.
I haue but one heart, and that hearts his due.
How can I then bestow the same on you?
Whilst he liues, his I liue, be it nere so poore,
And rather be his wife then a kings whore.
80   *Hammon.* Chaste and deare woman, I will not abuse thee,
Although it cost my life, if thou refuse me.
Thy husband, prest for France, what was his name?
 Iane. Rafe Damport.
 Hammon.   Damport? — Heres a letter sent
From France to me, from a deare friend of mine,
85 A gentleman of place; here he doth write
Their names that haue bin slaine in euery fight.
 Iane. I hope deaths scroll containes not my loues name.
 Hammon. Cannot you reade?
 Iane.   I can.
 Hammon.   Peruse the same.
To my remembrance such a name I read
90 Amongst the rest. See here.
 Iane.   Aye me, hees dead!
Hees dead! if this be true, my deare hearts slaine.
 Hammon. Haue patience, deare loue.
 Iane.   Hence, hence!
 Hammon.   Nay, sweete Iane,
Make not poore sorrow prowd with these rich teares.
I mourne thy husbands death, because thou mournst.

---

67. *and say* Fr.; *say,* however, imperative = *suppose.* — 68. *beleeue
you, constant* Qq. — 71. *hope* E. — 81. *me* om. DE. — 88. *Can you read*
CDE. — 93. *no poor* E.

Iane. That bil is forgde; 'tis signde by forgerie.　　95
Hammon. Ile bring thee letters sent besides to many,
Carrying the like report: Iane, tis too true.
Come, weepe not: mourning, though it rise from loue,
Helpes not the mourned, yet hurtes them that mourne.
Iane. For Gods sake, leaue me.　　100
Hammon.　　　　　　　　Wither dost thou turne?
Forget the deade, loue them that are aliue;
His loue is faded, trie how mine wil thriue.
Iane. Tis now no time for me to thinke on loue.
Hammon. Tis now best time for you to thinke on loue,
Because your loue liues not.　　105
Iane.　　　　　　　　Thogh he be dead,
My loue to him shal not be buried.
For Gods sake, leaue me to my selfe alone;
Hammon. Twould kil my soule, to leaue thee drownd in mone.
Answere me to my sute, and I am gone;
Say to me yea or no.　　110
Iane.　　　　　　No.
Hammon.　　　　　　　Then farewell.
One farewel wil not serue, I come again;
Come, drie these wet cheekes; tel me, faith, sweete Iane,
Yea or no, once more.
Iane.　　　　　　Once more I say: no;
Once more be gone, I pray; else wil I go.
Hammon. Nay, then I wil grow rude, by this white hand,　　115
Until you change that colde no; here Ile stand
Til by your hard heart —
Iane.　　　　　　Nay, for Gods loue, peace!
My sorrowes by your presence more increase.
Not that you thus are present, but al griefe
Desires to be alone; therefore in briefe　　120
Thus much I say, and saying bid adew:
If euer I wed man, it shall be you.

96. *too* D. — 100. *Whether* BC. — 101. *deede* A, *dead* BCDE. —
104, 105. One line in Qq.; divided by Fr. — 108. *thee*] *the* E. — 118. *your*]
you CDE.

Hammon.   O blessed voyce!   Deare Iane, lle urge no more,
Thy breath hath made me rich.

Iane.   Death makes me poor. *[Exeunt.*

SCENE II.

Enter HODGE, *at his shop-boord,* RAFE, FIRK, HANS, *and a boy
at work.*

All.   Hey, downe a downe, downe derie.

Hodge.   Well said, my hearts; plie your worke to-day, we
loytred yesterday; to it pell-mel, that we may liue to be Lord
Maiors, or Aldermen at least.

5   *Firke.*   Hey, downe a downe, derie.

Hodge.   Well said, yfaith!   How sayst thou, Hauns, doth
not Firk tickle it?

Hauns.   Yaw, mester.

Firke.   Not so neither, my organe-pipe squeaks this morning

10   for want of licoring.   Hey, downe a downe, derie!

Hans.   Forward, Firk, tow best un iolly yongster.   Hort, I,
mester, ic bid yo, cut me vn pair vampres vor mester Ieffres
bootes.

Hodge.   Thou shalt, Hauns.

15   *Firke.*   Master!

Hodge.   How now, boy?

Firke.   Pray, now you are in the cutting vaine, cut mee
out a paire of counterfeits, or else my ̄ worke will not passe
currant; hey, downe a downe!

20   *Hodge.*   Tell me, sirs, are my coosin Mrs. Priscillaes shooes
done?

Firke.   Your coosin? No, maister; one of your auntes, hang
her; let them alone.

---

124. [*Exit.*] C.
SCENE II. [*Scene* 13. *London. A street before Hodge's shop.*] Fr. —
1. *Hey down, a down, dery* BCDE. — 8. *meester* DE. — 11. *youngster* C.
— 12. *vãpres* AB, *vanpres* CDE; *effres* C, *Effres* DE. — 15. *Maister* C. —
19. *down a down dery* DE. — 20. *Mrs.*] *M.* Qq.; *Priscialles* B.; *Priscicalles*
C, *Priscillas* D, *Pricillas* E.

Rafe. I am in hand with them; she gaue charge that none but I should doe them for her.   25

Firke. Thou do for her? then twill be a lame doing, and that she loues not. Rafe, thou mightst haue sent her to me, in faith, I would haue yearkt and firkt your Priscilla. Hey, downe a downe, derry. This geere will not holde.

Hodge. How saist thou, Firke, were we not merry at Old-Ford?   30

Firke. How, merry? why, our buttockes went jiggy-ioggy like a quagmyre. Wel, Sir Roger Oatemeale, if I thought all meale of that nature, I would eate nothing but bagpuddings.

Rafe. Of all good fortunes my fellow Hance had the best.   35

Firke. Tis true, because mistris Rose dranke to him.

Hodge. Wel, wel, worke apace. They say, seuen of the Aldermen be dead, or very sicke.

Firke. I care not, Ile be none.

Rafe. No, nor I; but then my M. Eyre wil come quickly   40
to be L. Mayor.

Enter SIBIL.

Firke. Whoop, yonder comes Sibil.

Hodge. Sibil, welcome, yfaith; and how dost thou, madde wench?

Firke. Sib-whoore, welcome to London.   45

Sibil. Godamercy, sweete Firke; good Lord, Hodge, what a delitious shop you haue got! You tickle it, yfaith.

Rafe. Godamercy, Sibil, for our good cheere at Old-Ford.

Sibil. That you shal haue, Rafe.

Firke. Nay, by the masse, we hadde tickling cheere, Sibil;   50
and how the plague dost thou and mistris Rose and my Lord Mayor? I put the women in first.

Sibil. Wel, Godamercy; but Gods me, I forget my self, wheres Haunce the Fleming?

Firke. Hearke, butter-boxe, nowe you must yelp out some   55
spreken.

Hans. Wat begaie you? Vat vod you, Frister?

---

26. *be but a* DE — 28. *Precilla* CDE. — 34. *meale*] *meate* C, *meat* DE. — 52. *woman* C. — 54. *Flemming* DE. — 57. *Wat*] *Vat* C; *begaie gon vat vod gon* Qq.; *vod*] *bod* DE.

Sibil.   Marrie, you must come to my yong mistris, to pull
on her shooes you made last.

60   *Hans.*   Vare ben your egle fro, vare ben your mistris?

Sibil.   Marrie, here at our London house in Cornehill.

Firke.   Will nobodie serue her turne but Hans?

Sibil.   No, sir. Come, Hans, I stand vpon needles.

Hodge.   Why then, Sibil, take heede of pricking.

65   *Sibil.*   For that let me alone. I haue a tricke in my budget.
Come, Hans.

Hans.   Yaw, yaw, ic sall meete yo gane.

[*Exit* HANS *and* SIBIL.

Hodge.   Go, Hans, make haste againe. Come, who lacks
worke?

70   *Firke.*   I, maister, for I lacke my breakfast; tis munching
- time, and past.

Hodge.   Ist so? why, then leaue worke, Raph. To breakfast!
Boy, looke to the tooles. Come, Raph; come, Firke. [*Exeunt.*

SCENE III.

Enter a Seruing-man.

Serv.   Let me see now, the signe of the Last in Towerstreet.
Mas, yonders the house. What, haw! Whoes within?

Enter RAPH.

Raph.   Who calles there? What want you, sir?

Serv.   Marrie, I would haue a paire of shooes made for a
5   gentlewoman against to-morrow morning. What, can you do
them?

Raph.   Yes, sir, you shall haue them. But what lengths
her foote?

Serv.   Why, you must make them in all parts like this shoe;
10   but, at any hand, faile not to do them, for the gentlewoman
is to be married very early in the morning.

Raph.   How? by this shoe must it be made? by this? Are
you sure, sir, by this?

60. *Vare*] *Var* C, *War* DE. — 61. *Corne-waile* AB, *Cornwall* C,
Cornhill DE; cp. II. 1. 30.

SCENE III. Scene II and III form one scene in Fr.'s edition. -
3. *Who's* DE. — 7. *But* om. E.

Serv. How, by this? Am I sure, by this? Art thou in thy wits? I tell thee, I must haue a paire of shooes, dost thou 15 marke me? a paire of shooes, two shooes, made by this verie shoe, this same shoe, against to-morrow morning by foure a clock. Dost vnderstand me? Canst thou do't?

Raph. Yes, sir, yes — I, I, I can do't. By this shoe, you say? I should knowe this shoe. Yes, sir, yes, by this shoe, 20 I can do't. Foure a clocke, well. Whither shall I bring them?

Serv. To the signe of the Golden Ball in Watlingstreete; enquire for one maister Hamon, a gentleman, my maister.

Raph. Yea, sir; by this shoe, you say?

Serv. I say, maister Hammon at the Golden Ball; hee's 25 the bridegroome, and those shooes are for his bride.

Raph. They shal be done by this shoe; wel, well, Maister Hammon at the Golden Shoe — I would say, the Golden Ball; verie well, verie well. But I pray you, sir, where must maister Hammon be married? 30

Serv. At Saint Faiths Church, under Paules. But whats that to thee? Prethee, dispatch those shooes, and so farewel. [*Exit.*

Raph. By this shoe, said he. How am I amazde At this strange accident! Vpon my life, This was the verie shoe I gaue my wife, 35 When I was prest for France; since when, alas! I neuer could heare of her: it is the same, And Hammons bride no other but my Iane.

Enter FIRKE.

Firke. Snailes, Raph, thou hast lost thy part of three pots, a countrieman of mine gaue me to breakfast. 40

Rafe. I care not; I haue found a better thing.

Firke. A thing? away! Is it a mans thing, or a womans thing?

Rafe. Firke, dost thou know this shooe?

Firke. No, by my troth; neither doth that know me! I 45 haue no acquaintance with it, tis a meere stranger to me.

---

14. *I am sure* DE. — 18. *Dost*] *dost thou* BCDE; *Canst thou*] *Canst* CDE; *do it* BCDE. — 21. *Whether* C. — 27. *well, very well* CDE. — 28. *should* E. — 33. *I am* DE. — 37. *'tis the same* CDE. — 38. *but*] *than* DE.

 Rafe. Why, then I do; this shooe, I durst be sworne,
Once couered the instep of my Iane.
This is her size, her breadth, thus trod my loue;
50 These true-loue knots I prickt; I hold my life,
By this old shooe I shall finde out my wife.
 Firke. Ha, ha! Old shoo, that wert new! How a murren
came this ague-fit of foolishnes vpon thee?
 Rafe. Thus, Firke: euen now here came a scruing-man;
55 By this shooe would he haue a new paire made
Against to-morrow morning for his mistris,
Thats to be married to a gentleman.
And why may not this be my sweete Iane?
 Firke. And why maist not thou be my sweete asse? Ha, ha!
60 *Rafe.* Well, laugh and spare not! But the trueth is this:
Against to-morrow morning Ile prouide
A lustie crue of honest shoomakers,
To watch the going of the bride to church.
If she proue Iane, Ile take her in dispite
65 From Hammon and the diuel, were he by.
If it be not my Iane, what remedy?
Hereof I am sure, I shall liue till I die,
Although I neuer with a woman lie.   *[Exit.*
 Firke. Thou lie with a woman to builde nothing but
70 Cripple-gates! Well, God sends fooles fortune, and it may
be, he may light vpon his matrimony by such a deuice; for
wedding and hanging goes by destiny.   *[Exit.*

Scene IV.

Enter Hans *and* Rose, *arme in arme.*

 Hans. How happie am I by embracing thee!
Oh, I did feare such crosse mishaps did raigne,
That I should neuer see my Rose againe.

52. *were* CDE. — 58. *sweete* has the quality of a disyllable here; cp. Haml. I. 3. 8; *sweet* BCDE; *sweetest* Fr., but cp. Firke's answer. — 65. *Of Hammon* CDE. — 67. *am I* AB. — 68. *[Exit.]* om. CDE. — 72. *[Exit.]* om. C, *[Exeunt.]* DE.
 Scene IV. *[Scene 14. London. A room in Sir Roger's house.]* Fr. — 2 *such]* surh E.

Rose.   Sweet Lacie, since faire Oportunitie
Offers her selfe to furder our escape,   5
Let not too ouer-fond esteeme of me
Hinder that happie hower. Inuent the meanes,
And Ros. will follow thee through all the world.
    Han .   Oh, how I surfeit with excess of ioy,
Made happie by thy rich perfection!   10
But since thou paist sweete intrest to my hopes,
Redoubling loue on loue, let me once more
Like to a bold-facde debter craue of thee,
This night to steale abroade, and at Eyres house,
Who now by death of certaine Aldermen   15
Is Maior of London, and my master once,
Meete thou thy Lacie, where in spite of change,
Your fathers anger, and mine vncles hate
Our happie nuptialls will we consummate.

Enter SIBIL.

Sibil.   Oh God, what will you doe, mistris? Shift for your   20
selfe, your father is at hand! Hees coming, hees coming!
Master Lacie, hide your selfe in my mistris! For Gods sake,
shift for your selues!
    Haus.   Your father come, sweete Rose — what shall I doe?
Where shall I hide me? How shall I escape?   25
    Rose.   A man, and want wit in extremitie?
Come, come, be Hauns still, play the shoomaker,
Pull on my shooe.

Enter LORD MAIOR.

Hans.   Mas, and thats well remembred.
Sibil.   Here comes your father.
Hans.   Forware, metresse, tis vn good skow, it sal vel dute,   30
or ye sal neit betallen.
    Rose.   Oh God, it pincheth me; what wil you do?

5. *further* CDE. — 8. *thorow* DE. — 9. *surfet* CD. — 11. *interest*
DE. — 13. *debtor* CDE. — 16. *maister* C. — 17. *spight* BCDE. — 18. *father*
C. — 19. *w:*] *me* AB. — 22. *maister* C. — 30. *sal*] *full* C. — 31. *niet*
CDE; *bettallen* D, *bettalen* E.

Hans. (*Aside.*) Your fathers presence pincheth, not the shoo.

L. Maior.   Well done; fit my daughter well, and shee shall
35 please thee well.

Hans.   Yaw, yaw, ick weit dat well; forware, tis vn good
skoo, tis gimait van neits leither; se euer, mine here.

Enter a prentice.

L. Maior.   I do beleeue it. — Whats the newes with you?

Prentice.   Please you, the Earle of Lincolne at the gate
40 Is newly lighted, and would speake with you.

L. Maior.   The Earl of Lincolne come to speake with me?
Well, well, I know his errand.   Daughter Rose,
Send hence your shoomaker, dispatch, haue done!
Sib, make things handsome!   Sir boy, follow me.   [*Exit.*
45 *Hans.*   Mine vncle come!   Oh, what may this portend?
Sweete Rose, this of our loue threatens an end.

Rose.   Be not dismaid at this; what ere befall,
Rose is thine owne.   To witnes I speake truth,
Where, thou appoints the place, Ile meete with thee.
50 I will not fixe a day to follow thee,
But presently steale hence.   Do not replie:
Loue which gaue strength to beare my fathers hate,
Shal now adde wings to further our escape.   [*Exeunt.*

SCENE V.

Enter LORD MAIOR *and* LINCOLNE.

L. Maior.   Beleeue me, on my credite, I speake truth:
Since first your nephew Lacie went to France,
I haue not seene him.   It seemd strange to me,
When Dodger told me that he staide behinde,
5 Neglecting the hie charge the king imposed.

Lincolne.   Trust me, Sir Roger Otly, I did thinke

33. (*Aside.*) wanting in Qq. — 34 *my*] *wy* D. — 36. *wiet* DE. —
37. *niets* DE. — 39, 40. Printed as prose in Qq.; divided by Fr. — 41. *come
speak* Qq., *to* add. by Fr. — 45. *My father come* CDE. — 49. *appointst* DE.
— 53. *to* om. C.
    SCENE V. [*Scene 15.   Another room in the same house.*] Fr. —
6. *Otley* CDE.

Your counsell had giuen head to this attempt,
Drawne to it by the loue he beares your child.
Here I did hope to find him in your house;
But now I see mine error, and confesse,   10
My iudgement wrongd you by conceuing so.

    L. Maior. Lodge in my house, say you? Trust me, my Lord,
I loue your nephew Lacie too too dearely,
So much to wrong his honor; and he hath done so,
That first gaue him aduise to stay from France.   15
To witnesse I speake truth, I let you know,
How carefull I haue beene to keepe my daughter
Free from all conference or speech of him;
Not that I skorne your nephew, but in loue
I beare your honour, least your noble bloud   20
Should by my meane worth be dishonoured.

    Lincolne. (*Aside.*) How far the churles tongue wanders from
Well, well, Sir Roger Otley, I beleeue you,   [his hart.
With more then many thankes for the kind loue,
So much you seeme to beare me. But, my Lord,   25
Let me request your helpe to seeke my nephew,
Whom if I find, Ile straight embarke for France.
So shal your Rose be free, my thoughts at rest,
And much care die which now lies in my brest.

              Enter SIBIL.

    Sibil. Oh Lord! Help, for Gods sake! my mistris; oh,   30
my yong mistris!

    L. Maior. Where is thy mistris? Whats become of her?

    Sibil. Shees gone, shees fled!

    L. Maior. Gone! Whither is she fled?

    Sibil. I know not, forsooth; shees fled out of doores with   35
Hauns the shoomaker; I saw them scud, scud, scud, apace,
apace!

    L. Maior, Which way? What, Iohn! Where be my men?
Which way?

40   *Sibil.* I know not, and it please your worship.
  L. Maior. Fled with a shoomaker? Can this be true?
  Sibil. Oh Lord, sir, as true as Gods in heauen.
  Lincolne. Her loue turnd shoomaker? I am glad of this.
  L. Maior. A fleming butter-boxe, a shoomaker!
45 Will she forget her birth, requite my care
With such ingratitude? Scornd she yong Hammon
To loue a honnikin, a needie knave?
Wel, let her flie, Ile not flie after her,
Let her starue, if she wil; shees none of mine.
50   *Lincolne.* Be not so cruell, sir.

     Enter FIRKE *with shooes.*

  Sibil.   I am glad, shees scapt.
  L. Maior. Ile not account of her as of my child.
Was there no better obiect for her eies
But a foule drunken lubber, swill-bellie,
A shoomaker? Thats braue!
55   *Firke.* Yea, forsooth; tis a very braue shooe, and as fit as
a pudding.
  L. Maior. How now, what knaue is this? From whence
          comest thou?
  Firke. No knaue, sir. I am Firke the shoomaker, lusty
Rogers cheefe lustie iorneyman, and I come hither to take
60 up the prettie legge of sweete mistris Rose, and thus hoping
your worshippe is in as good health, as I was at the making
hereof, I bid you farewell, yours — — — — Firke.
  L. Maior. Stay, stay, sir knaue!
  Lincolne. Come hither, shoomaker!
65   *Firke.* Tis happie the knaue is put before the shoomaker,
or else I would not haue vouchsafed to come backe to you.
I am moued, for I stirre.
  L. Maior. My Lorde, this villaine calles us knaues by craft.
  Firke. Then tis by the Gentle Craft, and to cal one knaue
70 gently, is no harme. Sit your worship merie! Sib, your yong

   42. *as true as you are Lord Mayor* DE. — 44. *Flemming* DE. —
47. *an h.* CDE. — 51. *I'll not accompt* C; *as my* DE. — 53. *lubber*]
lubbery DE. — 60. *hoping that your* DE.

mistris — Ile so bob them, now my Maister M. Eyre is Lorde
Maior of London.

L. Maior. Tell me, sirra, whoes man are you?

Firke. I am glad to see your worship so merrie. I haue
no maw to this geere, no stomacke as yet to a red peticote.　75
　　　　　　　　　　　　　　　　　[Pointing to Sibil.

　　Lincolne. He means not, Sir, to wooe you to his maid,
But onely doth demand whose man you are.

Firke. I sing now to the tune of Rogero. Roger, my
felow, is now my master.

　　Lincolne. Sirra, knowst thou one Hauns, a shoomaker?　80

Firk. Hauns, shoomaker? Oh yes, stay, yes, I haue him.
I tel you what, I speake it in secret: Mistris Rose and he
are by this time -- no, not so, but shortly are to come ouer
one another with "Can you dance the shaking of the sheetes?"
It is that Hauns — *(Aside.)* Ile so gull these diggers!　85

L. Maior. Knowst thou, then, where he is?

Firke. Yes, forsooth; yea, marry!

Lincolne. Canst thou, in sadnesse —

Firke. No, forsooth; no, marrie!

L. Maior. Tell me, good honest fellow, where he is,　90
And thou shalt see what Ile bestow of thee.

Firke. Honest fellow? No, sir; not so, sir; my profession
is the Gentle Craft; I care not for seeing, I loue feeling; let
me feele it here; *aurium tenus*, ten pieces of gold; *genuum
tenus*, ten peeces of siluer; and then Firke is your man in　95
a new paire of strechers.

L. Maior. Here is an Angel, part of thy reward,
Which I will giue thee; tell me where he is.

Firke. No point! Shal I betray my brother? No! Shal I
proue Iudas to Hans? No! Shall I crie treason to my cor-　100
poration? No, I shall be firkt and yerkt then. But giue me
your angell; your angell shall tel you.

Lincolne. Doe so, good fellow; tis no hurt to thee.

Firke. Send simpering Sib away.

　　71. *them*] *then* A. -- 75. *to red* B. — 76. *his*] *this* DE. - 79. *maister*
C. — 85. *(Aside.)* added by Fr. — 94. *it*] *if* DE. — 104. *simp'ring*
CDE.

105   *L. Maior.* Huswife, get you in.   [*Exit Sibil.*

    Firke. Pitchers haue eares, and maides haue wide mouthes;
but for Hauns Prauns, vpon my word, to-morrow morning
he and yong mistris Rose goe to this geere, they shall be
married together, by this rush, or else tourne Firke to a
110 firkin of butter, to tanne leather withall.

    L. Maior. But art thou sure of this?

    Firke. Am I sure that Paules steeple is a handfull higher
then London stone, or that the Pissing-Conduit leakes nothing
but pure mother Bunch? Am I sure I am lustie Firk? Gods
115 nailes, doe you thinke I am so base to gull you.

    Lincolne. Where are they married? Dost thou know the
                               church?

    Firke. I neuer go to church, but I know the name of it;
it is a swearing church — stay a while, tis — I, by the mas,
no, no, — tis — I, by my troth, no, nor that; tis — I, by
120 my faith, that, that, tis, I, by my Faithes Church vnder Paules
crosse. There they shall be knit like a paire of stockings in
matrimonie; there theile be inconie.

    Lincolne. Vpon my life, my nephew Lacie walkes
In the disguise of this Dutch shoomaker.

125   *Firke.* Yes, forsooth.

    Lincolne. Doth he not, honest fellow?

    Firke. No, forsooth; I thinke Hauns is nobodie but Hans,
no spirite.

    L. Maior. My mind misgiues me now, tis so, indeede.

130   *Lincolne.* My cosen speakes the language, knowes the trade.

    L. Maior. Let me request your companie, my Lord;
Your honourable presence may, no doubt,
Refraine their head-strong rashnesse, when my selfe
Going alone perchance may be oreborne.

135 Shall I request this fauour?

    Lincolne.   This, or what else.

    Firke. Then you must rise betimes, for they meane to fall

---

105. Stage-dir. wanting in CDE. — 107. *prauns* AB, *praunse* C,
praunce DE. — 115. *'snails* C, *'snailes* DE. — 120. *Chuch* A. — 121. *of*
om. B; *stockins* DE. — 122. *in conie,* or, *in cony* Qq. — 123. *Linc.* om.
E. — 126. *Does* CD; *honest shoemaker* CD.

to their hey-passe and repasse, pindy-pandy, which hand
will you haue, very carely.

   L. Maior. My care shal euery way equal their haste.
This night accept your lodging in my house,   140
The earlier shal we stir, and at Saint Faithes
Preuent this giddy hare-braind nuptiall.
This trafficke of hot loue shal yeeld cold gaines:
They ban our loues, and weele forbid their baines. *[Exit.*

   Lincolne. At Saint Faithes Church thou saist?   145
   Firke. Yes, by their troth.
   Lincolne. Be secret, on thy life.   *[Exit.*
   Firke. Yes, when I kisse your wife! Ha, ha, heres no
craft in the Gentle Craft. I came hither of purpose with
shooes to Sir Rogers worship, whilst Rose, his daughter, be 150
coniecatcht by Hauns. Soft nowe; these two gulles will be
at Saint Faithes Church to-morrow morning, to take master
Bridegroome and mistris Bride napping, and they, in the
meane time, shal chop vp the matter at the Sauoy. But the
best sport is, Sir Roger Otly will find my felow lame Rafes 155
wife going to marry a gentleman, and then heele stop her
insteede of his daughter. Oh braue! there wil be fine tickling
sport. Soft now, what haue I to doe? Oh, I know; now a
messe of shoomakers meate at the Wooll-Sack in Ivie lane,
to cozen my gentleman of lame Rafes wife, thats true.   160

         Alacke, alacke!
         Girles, holde out tacke!
         For nowe smockes for this iumbling
         Shall goe to wracke.   *[Exit.*

ACT V.

Scene 1.

Enter AYRE, *his* WIFE, HAUNS, *and* ROSE.

   Eyre. This is the morning, then; stay, my bully, my honest
Hauns, is it not?

   137. *hey pasta* BC; *pindy pany* BC. — 144. [*Exeunt.*] AB. — 146. Qy.
read, *by my troth.* — 148. *Yet* DE. — 152. *maste* B, *maister* C. — 154. *meane*]
nean E; *at*] *of* E. — 155. *Otley* CDE; *fellow lame*, *Rafes wife* Qq. —
161—164. Printed as prose in Qq., divided by Fr.
   ACT V. SCENE I. [*Scene 16. A room in Eyre's house.*] Fr.

Hans. This is the morning that must make vs two happy
or miserable; therefore, if you —

5   *Eyre.* Away with these iffes and ands, Hauns, and these
et cacteraes! By mine honor, Rowland Lacie, none but the
king shall wrong thee. Come, feare nothing, am not I Sim
Eyre? Is not Sim Eyre Lord Mayor of London? Feare
nothing, Rose: let them al say what they can; dainty, come

10   thou to me — laughest thou?

Wife. Good my Lord, stand her friend in what thing you may.

Eyre. Why, my sweete Lady Madgy, thincke you Simon
Eyre can forget his fine Dutch Iourneyman? No, vah! Fie,
I scorne it, it shall neuer be cast in my teeth, that I was un-

15   thankeful. Lady Madgy, thou hadst neuer coverd thy Saracens
head with this french flappe, nor loaden thy bumme with
this farthingale, tis trash, trumpery, vanity; Simon Eyre had
neuer walkte in a redde petticoate, nor wore a chaine of golde,
but for my fine journeymans portigues — And shall I leaue

20   him? No! Prince am I none, yet beare a princely minde.

Hans. My Lorde, tis time for vs to part from hence.

Eyre. Lady Madgy, Lady Madgy, take two or three of my
pie - crust - eaters, my buffe - ierkin varlets, that doe walke in
blacke gownes at Simon Eyres heeles; take them, good Lady

25   Madgy; trippe and goe, my browne queene of perriwigs, with
my delicate Rose and my iolly Rowland to the Sauoy; see
them linckte, countenance the marriage; and when it is done,
cling, cling together, you Hamborow Turtle - Doues. Ile beare
you out, come to Simon Eyre; come, dwell with me, Hauns,

30   thou shalt eate mincde pies and marchpane. Rose, away,
cricket; trippe and goe, my Lady Madgy, to the Sauoy;
Hauns, wed, and to bed; kisse, and away! Go, vanish!

Wife. Farewel, my Lord.

Rose. Make haste, sweete loue.

Wife.   Sheede faine the deede were done.

35   *Hauns.* Come, my sweete Rose; faster than deere weele run.

                                             [*They goe out.*

6. *celeraes* CDE. — 9. *say all* DE. — 12. *Maggy* DE. — 15. *Maggy*
DE; *hast* E; *covered* CD. — 21. *for vs* om. DE. — 22. *Lady Maggy,
Lady Maggy* DE. — 25. *Maggy* DE. — 28. *Hanborow* DE. — 31. *Magy*
C, *Maggy* DE. — 35. [*Exeunt.*] CDE.

Eyre. Goe, vanish, vanish! Avaunt, I say! By the Lorde of Ludgate, its a madde life to be a Lorde Mayor; its a stirring life, a fine life, a veluet life, a carefull life. Well, Simon Eyre, yet set a good face on it, in the honor of Sainct Hugh. Soft, the king this day comes to dine with me, to see 40 my new buildings; his maiesty is welcome, he shal haue good cheere, delicate cheere, princely cheere. This day, my fellow prentises of London come to dine with me too, they shall haue fine cheere, gentlemanlike cheere. I promised the mad Cappadocians, when we all serued at the Conduit together, 45 that if euer I came to be Mayor of London, I would feast them al, and Ile doot, Ile doot, by the life of Pharaoh; by this beard, Sim Eire wil be no flincher. Besides I haue pro-curd that vpon euery Shroue-Tuesday, at the sound of the pancake bell, my fine dapper Assyrian lads shall clap vp their 50 shop windows, and away. This is the day, and this day they shall doot, they shall doot.

Boyes, that day are you free, let masters care,
And prentises shall pray for Simon Eyre.   [*Exit.*

SCENE II.

Enter HODGE, FIRKE, RAFE, *and fiue or six shoomakers,*
all with cudgels or such weapons.

Hodge. Come, Rafe; stand to it, Firke. My masters, as we are the braue bloods of the shoomakers, heires apparant to Saint Hugh, and perpetuall benefactors to all good fellowes, thou shalt haue no wrong; were Hammon a king of spades, he should not delue in thy close without thy sufferaunce. 5 But tell me, Rafe, art thou sure tis thy wife?

Rafe. Am I sure this is Firke? This morning, when I strokte on her shooes, I lookte vpon her, and she vpon me, and sighed, askte me, if euer I knew one Rafe. Yes, sayde I. For his sake, saide she — teares standing in her eyes — 10 and for thou art somewhat like him, spend this peece of golde. I tooke it; my lame leg and my trauel beyond sea made me vnknown. All is one for that: I know shees mine.

37. *tis* E. — 45. *Cappidocians* A. — 50. *Assirian* DE. — 53. *maisters* C. SCENE II. [*Scene 17. A street near Saint Faith's Church.*] Fr. Stage-dir. *Frike* D; *Shoomaker* C. — 11. *for that thou* DE.

Firke. Did she giue thee this gold? O glorious glittering
15 gold! Shees thine owne, tis thy wife, and she loues thee;
for Ile stand toot, theres no woman will giue golde to any
man, but she thinkes better of him, than she thinkes of them
she giues siluer to. And for Hamon, neither Hamon nor
hangman shall wrong thee in London. Is not our olde
20 maister Eire Lord Mayor? Speake, my hearts.
     All. Yes, and Hamon shall know it to his cost.

          Enter HAMON, *his* MAN, IANE *and others.*

Hodge. Peace, my bullies; yonder they come.
Rafe. Stand toot, my heartes. Firke, let me speake first.
Hodge. No, Rafe, let me. — Hammon, whither away so
25 earely?
     Hammon. Vnmannerly, rude slaue, whats that to thee?
     Firke. To him, Sir? Yes, sir, and to me, and others.
Good morrow, Iane, how doost thou? Good Lord, how the
world is changed with you! God be thanked!
30 *Hammon.* Villaines, handes off! Howe dare you touch my
                                        loue?
     All. Villaines? Downe with them! Cry clubs for pren-
tises!
     Hodge. Hold, my hearts! Touch her, Hamon? Yea,
and more than that: weele carry her away with vs. My
35 maisters and gentlemen, neuer draw your bird-spittes; shooemakers are steele to the backe, men euery inch of them, al
spirite.
     All of Hammons side. Wel, and what of all this?
     Hodge. Ile shew you. — Iane, dost thou know this man?
40 Tis Rafe, I can tell thee; nay, tis he in faith, though he be
lamde by the warres. Yet looke not strange, but run to him,
fold him about the necke and kisse him.
     Iane. Liues then my husband? Oh God, let me go,
Let me embrace my Rafe.
     Hammon.   What meanes my Iane?
45 *Iane.* Nay, what meant you, to tell me, he was slaine?

---

21. Stage-dir. *and Iane* CDE. — 31. *prentizies* E. — 38. *Hamon
side* C. — 45. *you*] *yon* A.

Hammon.   Pardon me, deare loue, for being misled.
(*To Rafe.*) Twas rumourd here in London, thou wert dead.

Firke.   Thou seest he liues. Lasse, goe, packe home with
him. Now, M. Hamon, wheres your mistris, your wife?

Serv.   Swounds, M., fight for her! Will you thus lose her?   50

All.   Downe with that creature! Clubs! Downe with him!

Hodge.   Hold, hold!

Hammon.   Hold, foole! Sirs, he shal do no wrong.
Wil my Iane leaue me thus, and breake her faith?

Firke.   Yea, sir! She must, sir! She shal, sir! What   55
then? Mend it!

Hodge.   Hearke, fellow Rafe, followe my counsel: set the
wench in the midst, and let her chuse her man, and let her
be his woman.

Iane.   Whom should I choose? Whom should my thoughts   60
                                        affect
But him whom heauen hath made to be my loue?
Thou art my husband, and these humble weedes
Makes thee more beautiful then all his wealth.
Therefore, I wil but put off his attire,
Returning it into the owners hand,   65
And after euer be thy constant wife.

Hodge.   Not a ragge, Iane! The law's on our side; he that
sowes in another mans ground, forfets his haruest. Get thee
home, Rafe; follow him, Iane; he shall not haue so much as
a buske-point from thee.   70

Firke.   Stand to that, Rafe; the appurtenances are thine
owne. Hammon, looke not at her!

Serv.   O, swounds, no!

Firke.   Blew coate, be quiet, weele giue you a new liuerie
else; weele make Shroue Tuesday Saint Georges Day for you.   75
Looke not, Hammon, leare not! Ile firke you! For thy head
now, one glance, one sheepes eie, any thing at her! Touch
not a ragge, least I and my brethren beate you to clowtes.

46. *Parden* E; *O pardon* Fr., but *pardon* is to be pronounced as a
trisyllable. — 47. (*To Rafe*) added by Fr. — 50. *thus* om. E. — 55. *Yer*
C, *Yes* DE. — 63. *Make* DE. — 66. *euer after* DE. — 68. *a other* E. —
73. *sounds* E.

    Serv. Come, master Hammon, theres no striuing here.

80   *Hammon.* Good fellowes, heare me speake; and, honest Rafe,
Whom I haue iniured most by louing Iane,
Marke what I offer thee: here in faire gold
Is twentie pound, Ile giue it for thy Iane;
If this content thee not, thou shalt haue more.

85   *Hodge.* Sell not thy wife, Rafe; make her not a whore.
    Hammon. Say, wilt thou freely cease thy claime in her,
And let her be my wife?
    All.   No, do not, Rafe.
    Rafe. Sirra, Hammon, Hammon, dost thou thinke, a shooe-
maker is so base to be a bawde to his owne wife for com-
90 moditie? Take thy golde, choake with it! Were I not lame,
I would make thee eate thy words.
    Firke. A shoomaker sell his flesh and bloud? Oh indignitie!
    Hodge. Sirra, take vp your pelfe, and be packing.
    Hammon. I wil not touch one pennie, but in liew
95 Of that great wrong I offered thy Iane,
To Iane and thee I giue that twentie pound.
Since I haue faild of her, during my life,
I vow, no woman else shall be my wife.
Farewell, good fellowes of the Gentle Trade:
100 Your morning mirth my mourning day hath made. [*Exeunt.*
    Firke. (*To the Serving-man.*) Touch the gold, creature, if you
dare! Y'are best be trudging. Here, Iane, take thou it. Now
lets home, my hearts.
    Hodge. Stay! Who comes here? Iane, on againe with thy
105 maske!

      Enter LINCOLNE, LORD MAIOR *and* SERUANTS.
    Lincolne. Yonders the lying varlet mockt us so.
    L. Maior. Come hither, sirra!
    Firke. I, sir? I am sirra? You meane me, do you not?
    Lincolne. Where is my nephew married?
110   *Firke.* Is he married? God giue him ioy, I am glad of it.
They haue a faire day, and the signe is in a good planet,
Mars in Venus.

    79. *maister* C. — 100. *mornings mirth* A; [*Exit.*] BCDE. —
101. (*To the S.*) add. by Edd. — 111. *in* om. E.

L. Maior. Villaine, thou toldst me that my daughter Rose
This morning should be married at Saint Faithes;
We haue watcht there these three houres at the least,   115
Yet see we no such thing.

Firke. Truly, I am sorie for't; a bride's a prettie thing.

Hodge. Come to the purpose. Yonder's the bride and
bridegroome you looke for, I hope. Though you be Lordes,
you are not to barre by your authoritie men from women; 120
are you?

L. Maior. See, see, my daughters maskt.

Lincolne.   True, and my nephew,
To hide his guilt, counterfeits him lame.

Firke. Yea, truely; God helpe the poore couple, they are
lame and blind.   125

L. Maior. Ile case her blindnes.

Lincolne.   Ile his lamenes cure.

Firke. Lie downe, sirs, and laugh! My felow Rafe is taken
for Rowland Lacy, and Iane for mistris damaske Rose. This
is al my knauery.

L. Maior. What, haue I found you, minion?   130

Lincolne.   O base wretch!
Nay, hide thy face, the horror of thy guilt
Can hardly be washt off. Where are thy powers?
What battels haue you made? O yes, I see,
Thou foughtst with Shame, and shame hath conquerd thee.
This lamenesse wil not serue.   135

L. Maior.   Unmaske your selfe.

Lincolne. Leade home your daughter.

L. Maior.   Take your nephew hence.

Rafe. Hence! Swounds, what meane you? Are you mad?
I hope you cannot inforce my wife from me. Wheres Hamon?

L. Maior. Your wife?

Lincolne. What, Hammon?   140

Rafe. Yea, my wife; and, therefore, the proudest of you
that laies hands on her first, Ile lay my crutch crosse his pate.

Firke. To him, lame Rafe! Heres braue sport!

---

123. *guilt now* Fr. — 126. *blindnesse* D. — 138. *enforce* CDE. —
142. *lays hand* C.

Rafe. Rose call you her? Why, her name is Iane. Looke
145 here else; do you know her now?   [*Unmasking* IANE.
    Lincolne. Is this your daughter?
    L. Maior.   No, nor this your nephew.
My Lord of Lincolne, we are both abusde
By this base, craftie varlet.
    Firke. Yea, forsooth, no varlet; forsooth, no base; forsooth,
150 I am but meane; no craftie neither, but of the Gentle Craft.
    L. Maior. Where is my daughter Rose? Where is my child?
    Lincolne. Where is my nephew Lacie married?
    Firke. Why, here is good lacde mutton, as I promist you.
    Lincolne. Villaine, Ile haue thee punisht for this wrong.
155   *Firke.* Punish the iornyman villaine, but not the iorneyman Shoomaker.

                Enter DODGER.

    Dodger. My Lord, I come to bring vnwelcome newes.
Your nephew Lacie and your daughter Rose
Earely this morning wedded at the Sauoy,
160 None being present but the Ladie Mairesse.
Besides I learnt among the officers,
The Lord Maior vowes to stand in their defence
Gainst any that shal seeke to crosse the match.
    Lincolne. Dares Eyre the shoomaker vphold the deede?
165   *Firke.* Yes, sir, shoomakers dare stand in a womans quarrel,
I warrant you, as deepe as another, and deeper too.
    Dodger. Besides, his Grace to-day dines with the Maior;
Who on his knees humbly intends to fall
And beg a pardon for your nephewes fault.
170   *Lincolne.* But Ile preuent him! Come, Sir Roger Oteley;
The king wil doe us iustice in this cause.
How ere their hands haue made them man and wife,
I wil disioine the match, or loose my life.   [*Exeunt.*
    Firke. Adue, monsieur Dodger! Farewel, fooles! Ha,
175 ha! Oh, if they had staide, I would haue so lambde ·
them with floutes! O heart, my codpeece-point is readie

    145. Stage-dir. added by Fr. — 150. *not crafty* CDE. — 153. *promise*
E. — 166. *you* om. CDE. — 170. *Otley* CDE. — 175. *lambe* B.

to flie in peeces euerie time I thinke vpon mistris Rose; but
let that passe, as my Ladie Mairesse saies.

Hodge. This matter is answerd. Come, Rafe; home with thy
wife. Come, my fine shoomakers, lets to our masters, the new 180
Lord Maior, and there swagger this Shroue-Tuesday. Ile
promise you wine enough, for Madge keepes the seller.

All. O rare! Madge is a good wench.

Firke. And Ile promise you meate enough, for simpring
Susan keepes the larder. Ile leade you to victuals, my braue 185
souldiers; follow your captaine. O braue! Hearke, hearke!

                                    [*Bell ringes.*

All. The pancake-bell rings, the pancake-bel! Tri-lill,
my hearts!

Firke. Oh braue! Oh sweete bell! O delicate pancakes!
Open the doores, my hearts, and shut vp the windowes! keepe 190
in the house, let out the pancakes! Oh rare, my heartes!
Lets march together for the honor of Saint Hugh to the
great new hall in Gratious-streete-corner, which our maister,
the newe Lord Maior, hath built.

Rafe. O the crew of good fellows that wil dine at my 195
Lord Maiors cost to-day!

Hodge. By the Lord, my Lord Maior is a most braue man.
How shal prentises be bound to pray for him and the honour
of the gentlemen shoomakers! Lets feede and be fat with
my Lordes bountye.   200

Firke. O musical bel, stil! O Hodge, O my brethren!
Theres cheere for the heauens: venson-pasties walke vp and
down piping hote, like sergeants; beefe and brewesse comes
marching in drie-fattes; fritters and pancakes comes trowling
in in wheele-barrowes; hennes and orenges hopping in porters 205
-baskets, colloppes and egges in scuttles, and tartes and
custardes comes quauering in in mault-shouels.

---

185. *Sue keeps* F. — 187. *pancake-ball* B. — 190. *door* BCDE. —
197. *The Lord Mayor is* CDE. — 198. *honor* C. — 200. *my Lord Mayor's
bounty* CDE.   202. *venison* CDE; *pastimes* A. — 203. *hot* CDE. —
204. *come* BCDE; *in* om. BCDE; *drifattes* DE. — 205. *wheel-barrows* .,
barrowe B. — 206. *settles* B. — 207. *in* only once in BCDE.

Enter more prentises.

All. Whoop, looke here, looke here!

Hodge. How now, madde laddes, whither away so fast?

210 *First Prentise.* Whither? Why, to the great new hall, know you not why? The Lorde Maior hath bidden all the prentises in London to breakfast this morning.

All. Oh braue shoomaker, oh braue lord of incomprehensible good-fellowship! Whoo! Hearke you! The pancake

215 -bell rings.   [*Cast vp caps.*

Firke. Nay, more, my hearts! Euery Shrouetuesday is our yeere of jubile; and when the pancake-bel rings, we are as free as my Lord Maior; we may shut vp our shops, and make holiday. I'll haue it calld Saint Hughes Holiday.

220 *All.* Agreed, agreed! Saint Hughes Holiday.

Hodge. And this shal continue for euer.

All. Oh braue! Come, come, my hearts! Away, away!

Firke. O eternall credite to vs of the Gentle Craft! March faire, my hearts! Oh rare!   [*Exeunt.*

SCENE III.

Enter KING *and his Traine ouer the stage.*

King. Is our Lord Maior of London such a gallant?

Nobleman. One of the merriest madcaps in your land.
Your Grace wil thinke, when you behold the man,
Hees rather a wilde ruffin than a Maior.

5 Yet thus much Ile ensure your maiestie
In al his actions that concerne his state,
He is as serious, prouident, and wise,
As full of grauitie amongst the graue,
As any Maior hath beene these many yeares.

10 *King.* I am with child, til I behold this huffe-cap.
But all my doubt is, when we come in presence,
His madnesse wil be dasht cleane out of countenance.

208. *look here* only once in BCDE. — 209. *whether* BC. — 210. *Whether*
BE. — 212. *ooreakfast* B.
SCENE III. [*Scene* 18. *London. A street.*] Fr. — Stage-dir. *Enter
the king* CDE. — 4. *ruffian* DE. — 9. *this* DE.

Nobleman. It may be so, my Liege.

King.   Which to preuent,
Let some one giue him notice, tis our pleasure
That he put on his woonted merriment.   15
Set forward!

   All.   On afore!   [*Exeunt.*

SCENE IV.

Enter AYRE, HODGE, FIRKE, RAFE, *and other shoemakers,*
all with napkins on their shoulders.

Eyre. Come, my fine Hodge, my iolly gentlemen shooemakers; soft, where be these caniballes, these varlets, my
officers? Let them al walke and waite vpon my brethren; for
my meaning is, that none but shoomakers, none but the liuery
of my Company shall in their sattin hoodes waite vppon the   5
trencher of my Soueraigne.

Firke. O my Lord, it will be rare!

Ayre. No more, Firke; come, liuely! Let your fellowe
-prentises want no cheere; let wine be plentiful as beere, and
beere as water. Hang these penny-pinching fathers, that   10
cramme wealth in innocent lamb-skinnes. Rip, knaues, auaunt!
Looke to my guests!

Hodge. My Lord, we are at our wits end for roome; those
hundred tables wil not feast the fourth part of them.

Ayre. Then couer me those hundred tables againe, and   15
againe, til all my iolly prentises be feasted. Auoyde, Hodge!
Runne, Rafe! Friske about, my nimble Firke! Carowse me
fadome-healths to the honor of the shoomakers. Do they
drink liuely, Hodge? Do they tickle it, Firke?

Firke. Tickle it? Some of them haue taken their licour 20
standing so long that they can stand no longer; but for meate,
they would eate it, and they had it.

Ayre. Want they meate? Wheres this swag-belly, this greasie
kitchinstuffe cooke? Call the varlet to me! Want meat?

---

14. *him* om. E.
     SCENE IV. [*Scene* 19. *A great hall.*] Fr. — 17. *nimbly* C. — 18. *of*
Shoemakers CDE. — 24. *kitching stuffe* C.

25 Firke, Hodge, lame Rafe, runne, my tall men, beleager the
shambles, beggar all Eastcheape, serue me whole oxen in
chargers, and let sheepe whine vpon the tables like pigges
for want of good felowes to eate them. Want meate? Vanish,
Firke! Auaunt, Hodge!

30 *Hodge.* Your Lordship mistakes my man Firke; he means,
their bellies want meate, not the boords; for they haue drunk
so much, they can eate nothing.

Enter HANS, ROSE, *and* WIFE.

Wife. Where is my Lord?

Ayre. How now, Lady Madgy?

35 *Wife.* The kings most excelent maiesty is new come; hee
sends me for thy honor; one of his most worshipful peeres
bade me tel thou must be mery, and so forth; but let that
passe.

Eyre. Is my Soueraigne come? Vanish, my tall shoomakers,
40 my nimble brethren; looke to my guests, the prentises. Yet
stay a little! How now, Hans? How lookes my little Rose?

Hans. Let me request you to remember me.
I know, your Honour easily may obtaine
Free pardon of the king for me and Rose,
45 And reconcile me to my vncles grace.

Eyre. Haue done, my good Hans, my honest iorneyman;
looke cheerely! Ile fall vpon both my knees, till they be as
hard as horne, but Ile get thy pardon.

Wife. Good my Lord, haue a care what you speake to
50 his grace.

Eyre. Away, you Islington whitepot! hence, you hopperarse!
you barly-pudding, ful of magots! you broyld carbonado!
auaunt, auaunt, avoide, Mephistophilus! Shall Sim Eyre
learne to speake of you, Ladie Madgie? Vanish, mother
55 Miniuer-cap; vanish, goe, trip and goe; meddle with your
partlets and your pishery-pasherie, your flewes and your

25. *beleaguer* CDE. — 26. *begger* CDE. — 27. *charges* E; *table* C.
— 34. *Maggy* DE. — 43. *honor* C. — 44. *of*] *from* DE. — 45. *my*] *thy*
C. — 46. *honost* C. — 51. *happerarse* AB. — 53. *Mephastophilus* AB. —
54. *learne*] *leaue* AB; *speak* CDE; *Maggy* DE. — 55. *Minever* C. —
56. *platters* CDE.

whirligigs; go, rub, out of mine alley! Sim Eyre knowes how
to speake to a Pope, to Sultan Soliman, to Tamburlaine, and
he were here; and shal I melt, shal I droope before my
Soueraigne? No, come, my Ladie Madgie! Follow me, Hauns!   60
About your businesse, my frolicke free-booters! Firke, friske
about, and about, and about, for the honour of mad Simon
Eyre, Lord Maior of London.

   Firke. Hey, for the honour of the shoomakers.   [*Exeunt.*

SCENE V.

A long flourish, or two. Enter KING, NOBLES, EYRE, *his*
WIFE, LACIE, ROSE. LACIE *and* ROSE *kneele.*

   King. Well, Lacie, though the fact was verie foule
Of your reuolting from our kingly loue
And your owne ductie, yet we pardon you.
Rise both, and, mistris Lacie, thanke my Lord Maior
For your yong bridegroome here.   5

   Eyre. So, my deere Liege, Sim Eyre and my brethren, the
gentlemen shoomakers, shal set your sweete maiesties image
cheeke by iowle by Saint Hugh for this honour you haue
done poore Simon Eyre. I beseech your grace, pardon my
rude behauiour; I am a handicraftsman, yet my heart is   10
without craft; I would be sory at my soule, that my boldnesse
should offend my king.

   King. Nay, I pray thee, good Lord Maior, be euen as mery
As if thou wert among thy shoomakers;
It does me good to see thee in this humour.   15

   Eyre. Saist thou me so, my sweete Dioclesian? Then, hump!
Prince am I none, yet am I princely borne. By the Lord of
Ludgate, my Liege, Ile be as merrie as a pie.

   King. Tell me, infaith, mad Eyre, how old thou art.

   Eyre. My liege, a verie boy, a stripling, a yonker; you   20
see not a white haire on my head, not a gray in this beard.
Euerie haire, I assure thy maiestie, that stickes in this beard,

   58. *Somliman* C, *Solyman* DE; *Tamberlaine* CDE. — 59. *defore* E.
— 60. *Maggy* DE. — 62. *honor* C. — 64. *of Shoemakers* CDE.
   SCENE V. [*Scene 20. An open yard before the hall.*] Fr. — Stage-
dir. *the King* CDE. — 8. *jole* CDE. — 14. *thy*] *the* E. — 21. *nor a gray* DE.

Sim Eyre values at the king of Babilons ransome, Tamar
Chams beard was a rubbing brush toot: yet Ile shaue it

25 off, and stuffe tennis-balls with it, to please my bully king.

King. But all this while I do not know your age.

Eyre. My liege, I am sixe and fiftie yeare olde, yet I can
crie humpe! with a sound heart for the honour of Saint Hugh.
Marke this olde wench, my king: I dauncde the shaking of

30 the sheetes with her sixe and thirtie yeares agoe, and yet I
hope to get two or three yong Lorde Maiors, ere I die. I am
lustie still, Sim Eyre still. Care and colde lodging brings
white haires. My sweete Maiestie, let care vanish, cast it vppon
thy Nobles, it will make thee looke alwayes young like Apollo,

35 and crye humpe! Prince am I none, yet am I princely borne.

King. Ha, ha!
Say, Cornewall, didst thou euer see his like?

Nobleman. Not I, my Lorde.

Enter LINCOLNE *and* LORD MAIOR.

King.   Lincolne, what newes with you?

Lincolne. My gracious Lord, haue care vnto your selfe,

40 For there are traytors here.

All. Traytors? Where? Who?

Eyre. Traitors in my house? God forbid! Where be my
officers? Ile spend my soule, ere my king feele harme.

King. Where is the traytor, Lincolne?

Lincolne.   Here he stands.

45 *King.* Cornewall, lay hold on Lacie! — Lincolne, speake,
What canst thou lay vnto thy Nephewes charge?

Lincolne. This, my deere Liege: your Grace, to doe me
Heapt on the head of this degenerous boy   [honour,
Desertlesse fauours; you made choise of him,

50 To be commander ouer powers in France.
But he —

King. Good Lincolne, prythee, pawse a while!
Euen in thine eies I reade what thou wouldst speake.

23. *Tama* A. — 31. *yong* om. CDE. — 36, 37. One line in Qq.;
divided by Fr. — 45. *hold*] *hands* CDE.

I know how Lacie did neglect our loue,
Ranne himselfe deepely, in the highest degree,
Into vile treason —   55
    Lincolne.   Is he not a traytor?
    King.   Lincolne, he was; now haue we pardned him.
Twas not a base want of true valors fire,
That held him out of France, but loues desire.
    Lincolne.   I wil not beare his shame vpon my backe.
    King.   Nor shalt thou, Lincolne; I forgiue you both.   60
    Lincolne.   Then, good my Liege, forbid the boy to wed
One whose meane birth will much disgrace his bed.
    King.   Are they not married?
    Lincolne.   No, my Liege.
    Both.   We are.
    King.   Shall I diuorce them then? O be it farre,
That any hand on earth should dare vntie   65
The sacred knot, knit by Gods maiestie;
I would not for my crowne disioyne their hands,
That are conioynd in holy nuptiall bands.
How saist thou, Lacy, wouldst thou loose thy Rose?
    Hans.   Not for all Indians wealth, my soueraigne.   70
    King.   But Rose, I am sure, her Lacie would forgoe?
    Rose.   If Rose were askt that question, sheed say no!
    King.   You heare them, Lincolne?
    Lincolne.   Yea, my Liege, I do.
    King.   Yet canst thou find ith heart to part these two?
Who seeks, besides you, to diuorce these louers?   75
    L. Maior.   I do, my gracious Lord, I am her father.
    King.   Sir Roger Oteley, our last Maior, I thinke?
    Nobleman.   The same, my Liege.
    King.   Would you offend Loues lawes?
Wel, you shal haue your wills, you sue to me,
To prohibite the match.   Soft, let me see —   80
You both are married, Lacie, art thou not?
    Hans.   I am, dread Soueraigne.

---

53. *knew* E. — 71. *I'm* CDE. — 73. *them*] *then* BC. — 74. *And* CDE;
in heart C; *those* E. — 77. *Otley* C. — 79. *sued* CDE. — 81. *are thou* C.

King.   Then, vpon thy life,
I charge thee, not to call this woman wife.
    L. Maior. I thanke your grace.
    Rose.   O my most gratious Lord!
                             [*Kneele.*

85   *King.* Nay, Rose, neuer wooe me; I tel you true,
Although as yet I am a batchellor,
Yet I beleeue, I shal not marry you.
    Rose. Can you diuide the body from the soule,
Yet make the body liue?
    King.   Yea, so profound?
90 I cannot, Rose, but you I must diuide.
This faire maide, bridegroome, cannot be your bride.
Are you pleasde, Lincolne? Oteley, are you pleasde?
    Both. Yes, my Lord.
    King.   Then must my heart be easde;
For, credit me, my conscience liues in paine,
95 Til these whom I diuorcde, be ioynd againe.
Lacy, giue me thy hand; Rose, lend me thine!
Be what you would be! Kisse now! So, thats fine.
At night, louers, to bed! — Now, let me see,
Which of you all mislikes this harmony.
100   *L. Maior.* Wil you then take from me my child perforce?
    King. Why, tell me, Oteley: shines not Lacies name
As bright in the worldes eye as the gay beames
Of any citizen.
    Lincolne.   Yea, but, my gratious Lord,
I do mislike the match farre more than he;
105 Her bloud is too too base.
    King.   Lincolne, no more.
Dost thou not know that loue respects no bloud,
Cares not for difference of birth or state?
The maid is yong, wel borne, faire, vertuous,
A worthy bride for any gentleman.
110 Besides, your nephew for her sake did stoope
To bare necessitie, and, as I heare,

    91. *Faire maide, this bridegroome* Qq. Corr. by Fr. — 92. *Otley* C.
— 93. *Yes, my Lord, yes* Fr.; *Then*] *There* E. — 101. *Otley* C.

Forgetting honors and all courtly pleasures,
To gaine her loue, became a shooemaker.
As for the honor which he lost in France,
Thus I redeeme it: Lacie, kneele thee downe! —   115
Arise, Sir Rowland Lacie! Tell me now,
Tell me in earnest, Oteley, canst thou chide,
Seeing thy Rose a ladie and a bryde?

L. Maior. I am content with what your Grace hath done.

Lincolne. And I, my Liege, since theres no remedie.   120

King. Come on, then, al shake hands: Ile haue you frends;
Where there is much loue, all discord ends.
What sayes my mad Lord Maior to all this loue?

Eyre. O my liege, this honour you haue done to my fine
iourneyman here, Rowland Lacie, and all these fauours which   125
you haue showne to me this daye in my poore house, will
make Simon Eyre liue longer by one dozen of warme summers
more then he should.

King. Nay, my mad Lord Maior, that shall be thy name,
If any grace of mine can length thy life,   130
One honour more Ile do thee: that new building,
Which at thy cost in Cornehill is erected,
Shall take a name from vs; weele haue it cald
The Leadenhall, because in digging it
You found the lead that couereth the same.   135

Eyre. I thanke your Maiestie.

Wife. God blesse your Grace!

King. Lincolne, a word with you!

Enter HODGE, FIRKE, RAFE, *and more shoomakers.*

Eyre. How now, my mad knaues? Peace, speake softly,
yonder is the king.   140

King. With the olde troupe which there we keepe in pay,
We wil incorporate a new supply.
Before one summer more passe ore my head,
France shal repent, England was iniured.
What are all those?   145

117. *Otley* C. — 122. *so much* Fr., but *Where* may be pronounced
as a disyllable. — 123. *this*] *his* B. — 124. *this*] *the* DE. — 125. *fauour* C.
— 131. *honor* C. — 138. Stage-dir. *Rafe* om. BCDE. — 145. *are those* CDE.

Hans.   All shoomakers, my Liege,
Sometimes my fellowes; in their companies
I liude as merry as an emperor.

    King. My mad Lord Mayor, are all these shoomakers?

    Eyre. All shooemakers, my Liege; all gentlemen of the
150 Gentle Craft, true Troians, couragious Cordwainers; they all
kneele to the shrine of holy Saint Hugh.

    All shoomakers. God saue your maisty!

    King. Mad Simon, would they anything with vs?

    Eyre. Mum, mad knaues! Not a word! Ile doot; I war-
155 rant you. They are all beggars, my Liege; all for them-
selues, and I for them all, on both my knees do intreate,
that for the honor of poore Simon Eyre and the good of
his brethren, these mad knaues, your Grace would vouchsafe
some priuilege to my new Leden-hall, that it may be
160 lawfull for vs to buy and sell leather there two dayes a
weeke.

    King. Mad Sim, I grant your suite, you shall haue patent
To hold two market-dayes in Leden-hall,
Mondayes and Fridayes, those shal be the times.
165 Will this content you?

    All. Iesus blesse your Grace!

    Eyre. In the name of these my poore brethren shoomakers,
I most humbly thanke your Grace. But before I rise, seeing
you are in the Giuing vaine and we in the Begging, graunt
170 Sim Eyre one boone more.

    King. What is it, my Lord Maior?

    Eyre. Vouchsafe to taste of a poore banquet that standes
sweetely waiting for your sweete presence.

    King. I shall vndo thee, Eyre, only with feasts;
175 Already haue I beene too troublesome;
Say, haue I not?

    Eyre. O my deere king, Sim Eyre was taken vnawares

---

146. *company* E. — 150. *Troyàns* CDE. — 152. *All. God saue your
maisty, all shoomaker* AB; *Majesty* DE. — 155. *beggers* CDE. — 156. *intreat*
CD. — 159. *priuiledge* C. — 161. *in a week* CDE. — 162. *patten* B. —
163. *Leaden-Hall* CDE. — 169. *veine* CDE. — 172. *that's sweetly waiting*
BCDE. — 174. *feasts*] *this* BCDE. — 177. *O my dear* (*deare* DE) *king,
Sim Eyre cannot think* (*thinke* C, *say* DE) *so;* BCDE.

vpon a day of shrouing, which I promist long ago to the
prentises of London.

      For, and't please your Highnes, in time past,   180
      I bare the water-tankerd, and my coate
      Sits not a whit the worse vpon my backe;
      And then, vpon a morning, some mad boyes,
      It was Shrouetuesday, ecune as tis now,
Gaue me my breakfast, and I swore then by the stopple of 185
my tankerd, if euer I came to be Lord Maior of London, I
would feast all the prentises. This day, my Liege, I did it,
and the slaues had an hundred tables fiue times couered; they
are gone home and vanisht;

      Yet adde more honour to the Gentle Trade,   190
      Taste of Eyres banquet, Simon's happie made.
  King.   Eyre, I wil taste of thy banquet, and wil say,
I haue not met more pleasure on a day.
Friends of the Gentle Craft, thankes to you al,
Thankes, my kind Ladie Mairesse, for our cheere. —   195
Come, Lordes, a while lets reuel it at home!
When all our sports and banquetings are done,
Warres must right wrongs which Frenchmen haue begun.
                                        [*Exeunt.*

178 seqq. *upon a day of shroving which I promis'd* (*promist* CDE) *to all
the merry prentices* (*prentises* DE) *of London; for and't* (*an't* CDE) *please
you, when I was prentice* (*prentise* DE) *I bare etc.* BCDE. Probably, the
whole speech of Eyre was originally written in verse. — 187. *all* om. CDE. —
190. *honour*] *glory* CDE. — 190, 191. Printed as prose in AB. — 192. *Eyre*
om. CDE. — 197. *sportes*] *words* BCDE; *banquettings* C; *sports and*
om. E. — 198. *Warres*] *We* BCDE; [*Exeunt.*] om. CDE.

THE END.

NOTES.

Pag. 1. The art of shoemaking has been dignified with the title of 'the Gentle Craft', probably because the popular saints of the shoemakers, S. Crispin and S. Crispianus, are said to have been of noble birth, and even of royal blood.

Pag. 2. *Roger*, Eyre's journeyman, is in the course of the play sometimes called *Hodge*, the latter being a diminutive form of *Roger*; cp. Butler's Hudibras, Part II, Canto III, where Old Roger Bacon is called Old Hodge Bacon. Mr. Fritsche, therefore, is mistaken in supposing Roger and Hodge to be different persons. Nor does it appear from the play that Lovell is nephew to the Earl of Lincoln, as Mr. Fritsche describes him.

Pag. 3. 2 seqq. The somewhat irregular construction of the passage seems to be: *a Comedie, acted before the Queenes Maiestie, (and) graciously accepted by her Highnesse for the mirth and pleasant matter.* We have therefore thought it necessary to write *Maiestie, for* instead of *Maiestie. For* (Qq. and Edd.).

ib. 17. *Three-mens-song*, a song or catch for three voices; cp. *Three-man-song-men* Shak. Wint. IV. 3. 45. A *six-mens-song* is alluded to in Percy's Reliques, vol. II, p. 20 (Ed. Tauchnitz).

Pag. 4. 2. *Saint Hugh.* Sir Hugh, the son of a king of Britain, had, according to legend, become a shoemaker. In the time of Diocletian he was prosecuted for his faith, and finally put to death. While he was in prison, the journeymen-shoemakers were constant in their attentions to him, so that he wanted for nothing. In requital of their kindness, he bequeathed his bones to them, having nothing else to leave them. The shoemakers, consequently, stole the skeleton from the gibbet, and in order to turn the bones into profit and to avoid suspicion, they made them into tools (S. Hugh's bones). See the interesting little book: Delightful history of the Gentle Craft by Sam. S. Campion. Northampton, 1876.

Pag. 5. 8. *downe it* i. e. sing the burden of the song *down-a -down &c.*

12. *Ring compasse gentle ioy* Qq. and Edd. Perhaps: Spectators, embrace gentle joy, i. e. be merry and cheerful.

ACT I.

1, 27. *imbezeld.* To *embezzle,* spelled also *imbecile,* to waste, to dissipate in extravagance. Cp. Dryden, Persius' Sat.:

> *When thou hast embezzled all thy store,*
> *Wher's all thy father left?*

1, 54. *Deepe,* i. e. Dieppe.

1, 59. *Tuttle-fields,* i. e. Tothill-fields.

1, 77. *painted,* decked with artificial colours, false.

1, 88. *of France.* The conjecture, proposed in the Athenæum No. 1837 (Ian. 10, 1863), to read *fame* for *France,* seems not to be called for.

1, 90. *Portugues,* a gold coin worth about three pounds twelve shillings. See Ben Ionson, Alchemist, I. 1; ed. Cunningham, vol. II, p. 17 b.

1, 125. *pishery-pasherie.* Cp. the similar expressions *bibble -babble, gibble-gabble, prittle-prattle, twiddle-twaddle,* all meaning nonsensical talk.

ib. *of the best presence.* Cp. Shak. Per. I. 1. 9 *is't not a goodly presence* (German: *Erscheinung*).

1, 129. *with the mealy mouth.* *mealy,* soft as covered with meal; *a mealy mouth,* a voluble tongue.

1, 138. *cormorant.* Quibble with *colonel.*

1, 146. *occupied.* For the indecent meaning of the word, cp. Shak. 2 H. IV., II. 4. 160 seqq: '*These villains will make the word* [i. e. *captain*] *as odious as the word 'occupy', which was an excellent good word, before it was ill sorted.*'

1, 161. *your pols and your edipolls.* We regret to have to state that we have not been able to find out the exact meaning of this expression.

1, 162. *Midaffe,* either a corrupt spelling for *midwife,* term of contempt for a woman, or the same as *midriffe,* s. l. 137.

ib. *Cisly Bumtrincket,* a ludicrous denomination of a woman. It occurs again, used of a maid-servant II. 3. 36. Cp., besides, III. 4. 36 *I must enlarge my bumme.*

1, 165. *Too soone, my fine Firk, too soone!* Perhaps: Again you interrrupt me too soon!

1, 170. *Termagant* 'an imaginary God of the Mahometans, represented as a most violent character in old Miracle-plays and Moralities.' Schmidt, Shakespeare-Lexicon, s. v.

1, 171. *by the Lord of Ludgate.* Qy.: Did the hangman live at Ludgate?

1, 181. The common contempt and ill treatment which soldiers meet with, shall not affect him.

1, 188. *weake vessels,* i. e. women, as often in Shakespeare.

1, 210. Cp. Shak. Cor. I. 5. 5, 6 *that do prize their hours At a crack'd drachm.*

ib. *mustard tokens,* litt. spots on the body, as yellow as mustard and denoting the infection of the plague. Cp. the use of the German *Pestbeule.*

ACT II.

1, 5. *coronet* i. e. garland.

1, 18. *Lady of the Haruest,* cp. First Three-mans Song, l. 4 *Sweete Peg, thou shalt be my Summers Queene.*

1, 26. *out of cry* i. e. so that it cannot be called, out of estimation, wondrous.

1, 32. *mary gup.* Perhaps corrupted from *Marry, come up,* s. Shak. Rom. II. 5. 64, Per. IV. 6. 159, or a senseless exclamation, like *mary foh.*

1, 40. Qy.: *in thy gaskins?*

1, 43. *go by, Ieronimo, go by!* A phrase, taken from Kyd's Spanish Tragedy *(Not I Hieronimo, beware, go by, go by!)* and used as a sort of ἔπος πτερόεν by Elizabethan writers. Cp. Shak. Shr. Ind. 1. 8 *Go by, Saint Ieronimy,* and Webster and Dekker, Westward Hoe: *she's like a play; if new, very good company; but if stale, like old Jeronimo, go by, go by!*

1, 44 seqq. Cp. Middleton's Works, ed. Dyce, vol. II, p. 78: *Some foolish words she hath passed to you in the country, and some peevish debts you owe here in the city; set the hare's head to the goose-giblet, release you her of her words, and I'll release you of your debts, sir.'*

1, 51. *goe snicke up,* i. e. go and be hanged. Nares felt inclined to derive the word from 'his neck up'; more probably *snick* only conveys the idea of quick motion; cp. L. Germ. *schnicken* to move quickly, and s. Weigand II, 612. Generally, the phrase is *go snicke up;* but cp. Shak. Tw. II. 3. 101: *We did keep time, sir, in our catches. Sneck up.* See the ed. of W. A. Wright (Clar. Press Series), note ad loc., p. 112.

3, 4. *powder-beefe-queane,* a woman who sells powdered or salted beef, cp. l. 18 *sowce-wife.*

3, 10. *speake bandog and bedlam,* you are as loud as a fierce bandog, or as a lunatic.

3, 18. *sowee-wife*, a woman whose business it was to clean and pickle pigs' faces.

3, 42 seqq. 'There was a boor from Gelderland, — Merry they are; — He was as drunken he could not stand, — Drunken (?) they are. — Fill the can, — Drink, fair man.' The puzzling *upsolee* (l. 45) is perhaps the same as *upsee Dutch*, i. e. intoxicated (s. Nares s. v.). Hoffmann von Fallersleben emends the lines in this way:

> *Daer was een boer van Gelderlant,*
> *Vrolijkeit si bi hem!*
> *Hi was dronken, hi en cost· niet staen,*
> *Absolutie si bi hem!*
> *Tap eens het canneken,*
> *Drink schone manneken!*

(S. Elze, Die Engl. Sprache und Literatur in Deutschland, p. 18).

ib. *bombast-cotten-candle-queane*. Though we may understand compositions as *bombast-queane*, or *cotten-queane*, yet we are quite at a loss as to *candle-queane*, unless we are allowed to suppose *candle* to be another spelling for *kendal* (= *Kendal-greene*).

3, 50. *vplandish*, prop. belonging to the uplands, rustic; stranger.

3, 55 seqq. Mrs. Eyre's words have of course an ironical sense.

3, 57. *butter-boxe*, term of contempt for a Dutchman; s. III. 1. 146 seq.; it occurs again IV. 5. 44.

3, 66 seq. Servants, journeymen &c. were generally hired at St. Paul's; cp. Shak. 2 H. IV., I. 2. 58: *I bought him in Paul's, and he'll buy me a horse in Smithfield.*

3, 73. *gallimafric*, 'a hash of various kinds of meat' Webster.

3, 76. 'Good day, master, and your wife also.'

3, 80. 'Yes, yes, I am a shoemaker.'

3, 82. S. Hugh's bones are enumerated in the following lines, quoted by Campion, l. c., p. 35:

> *My friends, I pray you listen to me,*
> *And mark what S. Hugh's Bones shall be.*
> *First a Drawer and a Dresser,*
> *Two Wedges, a more and a lesser:*
> *A pretty Block three Inches high,*
> *In fashion squared like a Die,*
> *Which shall be call'd by proper Name*
> *A Heel-Block, ah, the very same:*
> *A Hand-leather and Thumb-leather likewise,*
> *To pull out Shooethread, we must devise;*

The Needle and the Thimble shall not be left alone,
The Pincers, the Pricking-Awl, and Rubbing-stone;
The Awl, Steel and Tacks, the sowing Hairs beside,
The Stirrop holding fast, while we sow the Cow-hide,
The Whetstone, the Stopping-Stick, and the Paring-Knife,
All this doth belong to a Iourney-man's Life:
Our Apron is the Shrine to wrap these Bones in;
Thus shroud we S. Hugh's Bones in a gentle Lamb's Skin.

3, 86. 'Yes, yes, be not afraid. I have all the things, to make shoes, great and small.'

3, 93. 'I do not know what you say; I do not understand you.'

3, 96. 'Yes, yes, I can well do so.'

3, 106. *trullibub* = trollop, a slattern, a slut.

3, 113. *an heele-block*, often mentioned among S. Hugh's bones, s. ad l. 82. Perhaps the block of wood on which the shoe was laid to hammer on the heel.

3, 114. 'Oh, I understand you; I must pay half a dozen cans; here, boy, take this shilling, tap once freely.'

3, 118. *my last of the fives.* Perhaps a particular term of the play, called the fives (?).

3, 125. *Clapper-dudgeon.* Nares: 'A cant term for a beggar. Probably derived from the custom of clapping a dish.' [*Clapdish* 'a wooden dish carried by beggars, with a movable cover, which they clapped and clattered to show that it was empty.'] Sim Eyre calls his wife so for 'her mealy mouth that will never tire'.

3, 127. *cunger*, conger ($\gamma\acute{o}\gamma\gamma\rho o\varsigma$) = sea-eel.

4, 6, *take soile*, a hunting term, prop. to resort to a marshy place (Fr. *souille*); thence, to take refuge anywhere.

4, 7. *embost*, panting and foaming from exertion. Cp. Shak. Shr. Ind. I. 17 *the poor cur is embossed;* Ant. IV. 13. 3 *the boar of Thessaly was never so embossed;* Milton, Sams. Ag. 1699 *As a dismayed deer in chase embost.*

5, 2. *Upon some no* and *Upon some I* (perhaps better printed *Upon some, no* and *Upon some, I*) seem to have been modish expressions of assertion, formed after *upon my word, upon my honour* etc.

ACT III.

1, 1 seqq. 'I shall tell you what, Hans; this ship that has come from Candia, is all full, by God's sacrament, of sugar, civet, almonds, cambric, and all things, a thousand thousand things. Take it,

Hans, take it for your master. There are the bills of lading. Your master Simon Eyre shall have good buying. What do you say, Hans?'

1, 9 seqq. 'My dear brother Firk, bring master Eyre to the Swan; there you will find this shipper and me. What do you say, brother Firk? Do it, Hodge. Come, shipper.' There were at that time two inns called the Swan in London, the one at Dowgate, the other in Old-Fish-Street. Cp. Drake, II, p. 133.

1, 25. *like S. Mary Overies bels.* 'East from the Bishop of Winchesters house, directly ouer-against it, stands a fair church called St. Mary over the Rie, or Overie, that is, over the water.' Stow's Survey of London (ed. William I. Thoms, London 1876), p. 151.

1, 29. *Sauce* = sauciness, Halliwell, Dict.

1, 47. 'The odd saying "a shoemaker's son is a prince born" may be held to be verified by the birth of a son to the legendary Prince Crispin and the Princess Ursula.' Delightful History, l. c., p. 32.

1, 53. *a vennentorie* = an inventory.

1, 61. *Finsbury.* 'A manor, north of Moorfields, famous for the exercise of archers. B. Ionson, Bartholomew-Fair: *Nay, sir, stand not you fix'd here, like a stake in Finsbury, to be shot at.'* Nares.

1, 66. *Tannikin*, a female Christian name, which sometimes occurs; cp. History of Tannakin Shinker (Lowndes, ed. Bohn, p. 2383, s. v. Shinker). Perhaps a diminutive form of Anne.

1, 67. *Eastcheape.* 'Little East Cheape, chiefly inhabited by basket-makers, turners, and butchers.' Stow, l. c., p. 79.

1, 81. *No more, Madge, no more.* Mrs. Eyre, hearing her husband ask for the odd ten, must be supposed to frown and look angry again. Fearing lest she should pour out again the phials of her wrath, Eyre tries to calm her by saying: *No more, Madge, no more.*

1, 104. *Skellum Skanderbag. Skellum*, Germ. *Schelm*, a scoundrel. *Skanderbag* or rather *Scander Beg* (i. e. Lord Alexander) is the name given by the Turks to Iohn Kastriota, the Albanian hero. Descending from the ancient kings of Albania, Scanderbeg freed his country from the yoke of the Turks, whose terror he was during a space of twenty-three years (1443—1467). The Turks deterred his bones, dealt them, and kept them as amulets. Cp. Childe Harold's Pilgrimage II. 38. 1 (ed. Darmesteter, p. 90).

1, 105. Firk means a ship from Cyprus and Candy and laden with silk and sugar.

1, 112. *beaten damaske.* Cp. *beaten silk* Marlowe, Dr. Faustus sc. IV, l. 17. What means the epithet *beaten?*

1, 113. Firk, assisting Sim Eyre in putting on the cassock and gown (l. 109), handles the clothes a little too roughly, and is checked by his master with the words: Soft, Firk; take care that you do not rear the nap of the cloth, and that you do not make my garments look threadbare.

1, 117. *giue you the wal*, i. e. give you precedence. Cp. Shak. Rom. I. 1. 15 *I will take the wall of any man or maid*.

1, 129 seqq. 'Good day, master. This is the shipper that has the ship of merchandize; the commodity is good; take it, master, take it.'

1, 134 seqq. 'The ship is on the river; there are sugar, civet, almonds, cambric, and a thousand thousand things, by God's sacrament; take it, master: you shall have good buying.' *reuere*, Dutch *revier*, French *rivière*.

1, 142. 'Yes, yes, I have drunk much.'

2, 9. Qy: *but no man?*

3, 24. *to fond my loue on*, i. e. to dote on. Cp. Shak. Tw. II. 2. 35 *And I, poor monster, fond as much on him*.

3, 56. *mammet*, or *mawmet*, from Mahomet, a puppet.

4, 9. Mrs. Eyre, of course, means to say the contrary.

4, 23. 'I thank you, mistress.'

4, 28. *backe-friend*, lit. a friend who stands at one's back, so that in case of need he does not act as a friend; thence, a false friend.

4, 29. 'Yes, I shall, mistress.'

4, 32. The corked shooes were high-heeled and continued in fashion amongst the ladies the greater part of the seventeenth century. Del. Hist., p. 57.

4, 39. Roger compares the flaps of the hood to the boards of a pillory. [*pillory*, 'a frame of wood erected on posts, with movable boards and holes, through which the head and hands of a criminal were formerly put to punish him.' Webster, s. v.].

4, 48. *a maske*. Cp. Shak. Gentl. IV. 4. 157—159:

> *But since she did neglect her looking-glass,*
> *And threw her sun-expelling mask away,*
> *The air hath starv'd the roses in her cheeks.*

4, 54. 'I am merry; may you be so' (lasst euch so sein).

4, 89. *ka me, ka thee*, a proverbial phrase, the origin of which is not quite clear. '*Ka me, ka thee, one good turne asketh another*.' Heywood's Poems (qu. by Nares). Cp. *Clawe me and Ile clawe thee*.

4, 115. *smugge up*, to render spruce, trim.

4, 125. 'Yes, my master is the great man, the sheriff.'

4, 132. *I smel the Rose.* 'The three - farthing silver-pieces of Queen Elizabeth had the profile of the sovereign with a rose at the back of her head.' Dyce, note to King John I. 143.

4, 139. 'See, my dear brother, here comes my master.'

4, 143. The flaps of the French hood are compared to a shoulder of mutton; cp. I. 39.

4, 148. *for twentie*, i. e. for the twenty Portuguese you lent me.

5, 18. *hunnie*, *honey* is used as a fond compellation also by Shak. Oth., II. 1. 206.

5, 21. *Ha, ha, ha* may either be what Prof. Elze calls a 'prosodical triplet,' i. e. three syllables spoken in the time of two (S. Kölbing, Engl. Studien IX. 267, 1885), or may be considered as the expression of a burst of laughter and stand for one syllable.

5, 27, 28. Better printed as prose; cp. IV. 5. 34, 35.

5, 65. 'I thank you, good maid.' *frister*, lit. a maid who is to be engaged *(Freierin)*; maid.

5, 75. *tickle it.* The same expression occurs IV. 2. 7; and cp. Shak. Troil., V. 2. 177.

ACT IV.

1, 69. 'I believe you behave yourself constant.'

2, 11—13. 'Forward, Firke, thou art a jolly youngster. Hark, ay, master, I pray you, cut me a pair of vampres for Master Ieffrey's boots.'

2, 12. *vampres*, usually *vamps*, upper-leather of a shoe. As the word is derived from Fr. *avant-pied*, it seems not to be necessary to introduce, as Mr. Fritsche does, *vamps* into the text.

2, 18. *counterfeits* 1) vamps; 2) false coin.

2, 57. 'What do you want (was begehrt ihr), what do you wish, frister?'

2, 60. 'Where is your noble lady, where is your mistress?'

2, 65. *I haue a tricke in my budget*, i. e. I have a trick *in petto*, I intend to play a trick.

2, 67. 'Yes, yes, I shall go with you.'

2, 68. *make haste again*, cp. *haste you again*, Shak. All's. II. 2. 74.

3, 31. *At Saint Faiths Church, under Paules.* 'At the west end of this Iesus chapel, under the choir of Paules, also was a parish church of St. Faith, commonly called St. Faith under Paul's, which served for the stationers and others dwelling in Paule's churchyard, Paternoster road, and the places near adjoining.' Stow, l. c., p. 123.

3, 70. *Cripple-gates.* 'Cripplegate, a place, saith mine author (Iohn Lidgate), so called of cripples begging there: at which gate,

it was said, the body (of King Edmond the Martyr) entering,
miracles were wrought, as some of the lame to go upright, praising
God.' Stow, p. 13.

3, 72. Cp. Shak. Merch. II. 9. 83: *Hanging and wiving goes
by destiny.*

4, 30, 31. 'Indeed, mistress, 'tis a good shoe; it shall well do it,
or you shall not pay.' As to *do it* cp. Shak. Lr. IV. 6. 90: *this
piece of toasted cheese will do't.*

4, 36, 37. 'Yes, yes, I know that well; indeed, it is a good
shoe, 'tis made of neat's leather; look here (?), sir.'

5, 8. Constr.: [*had*] *drawn* [*him*] *to it.*

5, 47. *honnikin.* Cp. *poor honey*, stupid fellow, simpleton.

5, 70. *Sit your worship merie.* Cp. *Rest you merry*, Shak. Rom. I.
2. 65, 86.

5, 84. The same expression occurs V. 5. 29.

5, 85. *digger*, lit. one who digs, i. e. one who sounds (or
'pumps') another person.

5, 96. The words *in a new paire of strechers* must be supposed to be spoken aside. *stretcher*, an outstretching of the truth,
a lie.

5, 106. *Pilchers have ears.* The same proverbial phrase occurs
in Shak. Shr. IV. 4. 52; R. III., II. 4. 37.

5, 110. *firkin*, a measure, the fourth part of a barrel.

5, 113. 'London Stone, now cased and preserved in the wall
of St. Swithin's Church, Cannon Street, to which it was removed
from the opposite side of the way, was the centre from which the
great roads radiated (i. e. the great military roads of the Romans)'
G. R. Emerson: London, How the Great City Grew, London 1862,
p. 9 seq.

ib. *Pissing-Conduit.* 'A small conduit near the Royal Exchange,
so called in contempt, or jocularity, from its running with a small
stream.' Nares. Cp. *The Pissing-conduit run nothing but claret wine.*
Shak. 2 H. VI., IV. 6. 3.

5, 122. *incony*, which occurs in Shak. L. L. L. III. 136 and
IV. 1. 144, is explained by Nares = sweet, pretty, delicate. Here
it seems to be = happy.

5, 137. *They meane to fall to their hey-passe and repasse.* 'You
must also haue your words of art, certaine strange wordes, that it
may not only breed the more admiration to the people, but lead
away the eye from espying ner of your conveyance, while you may
induce the mind to conceive, and suppose that you deale with
Spirits: and such kind of sentences, and od speeches, are used in
diuers manners fitting and correspondent to the action and feat
that you go about. As *Hey Fortuna, Furia, numquam, Credo, passe*

passe, when come you, Sirrah? or this way *hey Iack, come aloft for thy maisters aduantage, passe and be gone*, or otherwise, as *Alif, Casil: zaze, Hit, metmellal, Saturnus, Iupiter, Mars, Sol, Venus, Mercury, Luna?* or thus *Drocti, Micocti, et Senarocti, Velu barocti, Asmarocti, Ronnsec, Faronnsec. hey passe passe:* many such obseruations to this art are necessary, without which all the rest are little to the purpose.' The Art of Iugling or Legerdemain. By S. R. London, Printed by George Eld, 1614, p. 10. For more instances see Marlowe's Dr. Faustus, ed. Ward, note to sc. XI, l. 58.

5, 153. *napping*, i. e. kidnapping; cp. *to knab*, to lay hold of, or apprehend.

5, 161 seqq. In German: 'Ach, ach — Jetzt, ihr Mädchen, haltet Stand! — Denn jetzt werden in diesem Durcheinander — Hemden (i. e. Mädchen) in die Brüche gehen.'

ACT V.

1, 5. *Away with these iffes and ands, Hans.* Cf. The Spanish Tragedy (London 1618), Act II (Dodsley, Old Plays, ed. Hazlitt, vol. V, p. 40):

PEDRINGANO. *If Madame Belimperia be in love —*
LORENZO. *What, villaine, ifs and ands?*
PEDRINGANO. *Oh, stay, my Lord! she loves Horatio.*

1, 13. *vah*, a term used in music, = go on, continue, It. *va*, Fr. *va*.

1, 23. *pie-crust eater*, cp. beef-eater (for *buffetier*).

1, 45. *the mad Cappadocians.* St. George, the patron of England, is said to have been from Cappadocia.

ib. *Conduit.* Nares, s. v. *Tankard-bearer*: 'While London was imperfectly supplied with water, this very necessary office (of fetching water from the conduits or pumps in the streets) was performed by menial servants, or water-bearers; and in the families of tradesmen, by their apprentices. . . . These tankard-bearers, often assembling at the conduit in considerable numbers, were obliged to wait patiently each for his turn to draw the water.'

2, 4. *a king of spades*, roi de piques.

2, 31. *Cry clubs for prentises.* 'In any public affray, the cry was *Clubs, clubs!* by way of calling forth persons (particularly the London 'prentices) with clubs to part the combatants' [or to assist one party]. Nares.

2, 71. *appurtenances*, a law-term, that which belongs to something else; here the clothes and trinkets of Iane.

2, 74. Perhaps the 'blue-coats' were presented with new liveries on S. George's day. Cp. Nares s. v. S. George.

2, 93. *pelfe*, i. e. rubbish, money.

2, 153. *lacde mutton.* This passage corroborates Al. Schmidt's opinion (Shakespeare-Lexicon, s. v.), that *laced mutton* is not a cant term for prostitute, but only = woman's flesh, a petticoat, a smock.

2, 175. *lambde.* *to lamb* apparently means to treat somebody as a sheep, as a simpleton.

2, 187. 'Shrove-Tuesday, at whose entrance in the morning all the whole kingdom is unquiet, but by that time the clocke strikes eleven, which (by the help of a knavish sexton) is commonly before nine, then there is a bell rung, cal'd pancake-bell, the sound whereof makes thousands of people distracted, and forgetful either of manners or humanitie.' Iohn Taylor, quoted by Drake, Shakespeare and his Times, I, 151 seqq. — The Monday, preceding Shrove-Tuesday, was called Collop-Monday, from *collop* (l. 206), a piece of salted and dried meat.

3, 10. *I am with child,* i. e. I am anxious, impatient.

4, 26. *Eastcheape.* See note to III. 1. 67.

4, 51. *whitepot* 'a kind of food made of milk, cream, eggs and sugar, baked in a pot' Webster.

4, 55. *Miniver,* ermine, the fur of the ermine.

4, 56. *partlets,* bands or collars for the neck; *your flawes and your whirligigs,* ludicrous allusion to Mrs. Eyre's loquacity.

4, 57. *rub,* that which hinders motion or progress, obstacle.

4, 58. *Sultan Soliman.* An allusion to Kyd's Soliman and Perseda, published in 1599. Marlowe's Tamburlaine was published in 1590.

5, 85. *wooe,* 1) to solicit, 2) to court.

5, 134. *Leadenhall.* According to Stow, 'Leadenhall belonged in 1309 to Sir Hugh Nevill; in the year 1408, Robert Rikeden, of Essex, and Margaret, his Wife, confirmed to Richard Whittington, and other citizens of London, the said manor of Leadenhall. And in the year 1411, the said Whittington and other confirmed the same to the mayor and commonalty of London, whereby it came to the possession of the city. Then in the year 1443, the 21st of Henry VI., Iohn Hatherley, mayor, purchased licence of the said king to take up two hundred fother of lead, for the building of water conduits, a common granary, and the cross in West Cheape, more richly, for the honour of the city. In the year next following, the parson and parish of St. Dunston, in the east of London, seeing the famous and mighty man (for the words be in the grant, *cum nobilis et potens vir,*) Simon Eyre, citizen of London, among other his works of piety, effectually determined to erect and build a certain granary upon the soil of the same city at Leadenhall, of his own charges, for the common utility of the said city, to the amplifying and enlarging of the said granary, granted to Henry

Frowike, then mayor, the aldermen and commonalty, and their
successors for ever, all their tenements, with the appurtenances,
sometime called the Horsemill, in Grasse street, for the annual
rent of four pounds.   Also certain evidences of an alley and
tenements pertaining to the Horsemill adjoining to the said Leadenhall in Grasse street, given by William Kingstone, fishmonger, unto
the parish church of St. Peter upon Cornehill, do specify the said
granary to be built by the said honourable and famous merchant,
Simon Eyre, sometime an upholsterer, and then a draper, in the
year 1519.   He built it of squared stone, in form as now it show-
eth, with a fair and large chapel in the east side of the quadrant,
over the porch of which he caused to be written, *Dextra Domini
exaltavit me.'*   Cp., besides, the passages referring to Simon Eyre's
life in our Introduction.

www.ingramcontent.com/pod-product-compliance
Lightning Source LLC
Chambersburg PA
CBHW032157010726
47493CB00008BA/2725